The RAINBOW magic

WEATHER FAIRIES TREASURY

Special thanks to
Narinder Dhami,
Sue Bentley and
Sue Mongredien

ORCHARD BOOKS
338 Euston Road, London NW1 3BH
Orchard Books Australia
Level 17/207 Kent Street, Sydney, NSW 2000

First published as an abridged version by Orchard Books in 2009.

A CIP catalogue record for this book is available
from the British Library.

ISBN 978 1 40831 260 5

1 3 5 7 9 10 8 6 4 2

Printed in China
Orchard Books is a division of Hachette Children's Books,
an Hachette UK company

www.hachette.co.uk

The RAINBOW magic®

WEATHER FAIRIES TREASURY

by Daisy Meadows

Illustrated by Georgie Ripper

ORCHARD

The Fairyland Palace

Sweet Factory

Fores[t]

The Village Hall

River

Wetherbury Village

Jack Frost's Ice Castle

Green Wood

The Park

Mrs. Fordham's Cottage

Willow Hill

The High St.

The Museum

Kirsty's House

Fields

Yard

Mudhole

N
W — E →
S

Goblins green and goblins small,
I cast this spell to make you tall.
As high as the palace you shall grow.
My icy magic makes it so.

Then steal Doodle's magic feathers,
used by the fairies to make all weathers.
Climate chaos I have planned
on Earth, and here, in Fairyland!

Contents

Crystal
the Snow
Fairy

Chapter One

Crystal the Snow Fairy

"Do you think it will stay this sunny through the whole summer holiday?" Kirsty Tate asked, gazing out of the car window.

"Let's hope so," her mother replied. "Remember how changeable the weather was on Rainspell Island?"

Kirsty nodded. She and her parents had been to Rainspell Island in the last school break and Kirsty had made a new friend, Rachel Walker. The two girls now shared a special secret. They had helped the Rainbow Fairies get back to Fairyland, after Jack Frost had cast a nasty spell to banish them.

"Could Rachel come and stay, Mum?" Kirsty asked, as they drew up outside their cottage in the pretty village of Wetherbury.

"Yes, of course," Mrs Tate agreed. "Now, let's take the shopping indoors."

"OK," said Kirsty, getting out of the car. "Where's Dad?"

"I'm up here!"

Kirsty glanced up. To the left of the house was an old wooden barn. Mr Tate was standing at the top of a ladder repairing the leaky roof. Mrs Tate opened the car boot and handed two shopping bags to Kirsty.

As Kirsty carried them towards the house, something cold and wet landed on her nose. She stared as white flakes started falling from the sky. "It's snowing!" she gasped.

"Quick, go indoors!" called Mrs Tate, picking up the rest of the shopping.

Mr Tate was already climbing down from the ladder. They all rushed inside as the snow swirled around them.

"This is very strange," said Mr Tate, frowning.

Kirsty glanced out of the kitchen window. "The snow's stopped!" she cried.

Mr and Mrs Tate joined Kirsty at the window. The sun was shining now and a few puddles of water were all that remained of the sudden snowstorm.

"How extraordinary!" said Mr Tate. "Just like magic!"

Kirsty's heart began to thump. Could there be magic in the air?

"You'd better go and change out of that wet shirt, Kirsty," said her mum.

Kirsty turned away from the window. As she did so, she spotted an old weather-vane in the shape of a cockerel, lying on the kitchen table. "What's that?" she asked.

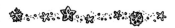

"I found it in the park this morning," her father said. "It will look great on top of the barn."

Kirsty reached out towards the weather-vane. As she did so, glittering sparkles danced towards her fingers. Kirsty blinked in surprise, and when she looked again, the sparkles had vanished. Feeling puzzled, she ran upstairs to her bedroom to change. There, on a shelf, sat the snow dome the fairies had given her. It was a special thank-you for helping the Rainbow Fairies, and Rachel had one just the same. When the snow dome was shaken up, glittering fairy dust swirled and sparkled.

But, right now, no one was shaking the snow dome – and yet the fairy dust was whirling around inside the glass! Kirsty stared at it. "It must be magic!" she told herself.

She dashed across the room and grabbed the glass dome, but dropped it straightaway; the snow dome was so hot it had burnt her fingers! As the dome fell, it struck the edge of the shelf and shattered. Sparkling fairy dust flew into the air around Kirsty and she found herself shrinking to fairy size, with glittering wings on her back! Suddenly, a strong breeze swept in through the open window. It picked up the fairy dust, whipping it into a whirlwind that swept Kirsty up and carried her out of the window!

Kirsty was whisked through the sky until the whirlwind brought her down close to the Fairy Palace. Kirsty saw King Oberon and Queen Titania waiting for her with a group of fairies and someone else Kirsty knew well.

"Rachel!" called Kirsty.

Rachel rushed over, as Kirsty landed on the grass. "I came the same way you did," she explained.

"Do you know why?" asked Kirsty. Rachel shook her head, as the King and Queen joined them.

"It's wonderful to see you both," beamed Queen Titania. "But I'm afraid we need your help again."

"What's happened?" asked both girls.

The King sighed. "I'm afraid that Jack Frost is up to his old tricks."

Rachel looked shocked. "But he promised not to harm the Rainbow Fairies anymore!" she said, shivering as the sun disappeared and it turned suddenly cold.

"Yes," Queen Titania replied. "Unfortunately, he didn't promise not to harm our *Weather* Fairies!"

"You mean this strange weather is all because of Jack Frost?" asked Kirsty, as sunshine blazed through the clouds once more.

The Queen nodded. "Doodle, our weather-vane cockerel, is in charge of Fairyland's weather," she explained. "Doodle's tail is made up of seven beautiful feathers – each feather controls one kind of weather."

"Every morning, Doodle decides on the best weather for every part of Fairyland," the King went on. "Then he gives each Weather Fairy the correct feather, and off they go to work."

"Come with us," said the Queen. "We'll show you what's happened."

The King and Queen led Rachel and Kirsty to a golden pool in the palace gardens. The Queen scattered some fairy dust onto the water, and a picture began to appear. It showed a handsome cockerel with a magnificent tail of red, gold and copper coloured feathers.

 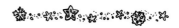
"That's Doodle," the Queen explained. "Yesterday he planned the weather for Fairyland, as usual."

"Jack Frost helps Doodle with the wintry weather," the King continued. "There's so much work, with all the ice and snow and frost. But now it's summer, Jack Frost has nothing to do."

"So he's bored," the Queen put in. "And that means trouble! Look…" She pointed at the pictures on top of the water. Doodle was standing on the palace steps.

Suddenly Kirsty gasped. "Look, Rachel!" she cried. "The goblins!" Rachel remembered Jack Frost's goblin servants. They were mean and selfish, with big feet and sharp noses. In the picture, seven goblins

were creeping towards Doodle. They reached out and snatched Doodle's tail feathers. Then, grinning and cheering, they ran away.

"Oh no!" said Kirsty, as the cockerel chased after the goblins. "Poor Doodle!"

The Queen sighed. "The goblins escaped into the human world, and Doodle followed them," she explained. "But without his magic feathers, and away from Fairyland, his strength failed."

"Doodle has become an ordinary weather-vane," the King said sadly. "We don't even know where he is now."

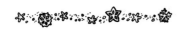 

"We need you to find the goblins," the Queen said, "so that we can get Doodle's tail feathers back. Until then, Doodle is stuck in your world, and our weather is topsy-turvy!" She looked up as a few raindrops fell. "The goblins are causing weather chaos for humans, too."

"Our Weather Fairies will help you," the King told the girls, introducing Crystal the Snow Fairy, Abigail the Breeze Fairy, Pearl the Cloud Fairy, Goldie the Sunshine Fairy, Evie the Mist Fairy, Storm the Lightning Fairy and Hayley the Rain Fairy.

"Pleased to meet you!" the fairies cried in silvery voices.

"Each Weather Fairy will help you to find her own feather," said the Queen. "And we know the goblins are hiding somewhere in Wetherbury."

"So that's why we had the snowstorm!" Kirsty exclaimed. "It was the goblins making mischief."

"What snowstorm?" asked Rachel.

Quickly Kirsty explained. "And I think I know where Doodle is, too," she added. "I think he's the weather-vane my dad found in the park!"

"Doodle is safe!" cried the Fairy Queen happily.

"But the snowstorm means that one of the goblins is nearby," the King warned, "with Doodle's magic Snow Feather!"

"Do you think your parents will let you come and stay with me?" Kirsty asked Rachel. "My mum says it's OK."

"I'll ask them," Rachel replied.

The King nodded. "That's a good idea," he said.

The Queen stepped forward. She had two shining golden lockets in her hand.

"Each locket is filled with fairy dust," she said, giving them to the girls. "You can use a pinch of this to turn yourself into fairies and back to humans again. But remember! Don't look too hard for magic — it will find you. And when you see it, you will know that one of the magic feathers is nearby."

The girls fastened the lockets around their necks.

"And beware of the goblins," the King added. "Jack Frost has cast a spell to make them bigger."

"Bigger!" Rachel repeated. "As big as humans?"

The King shook his head. "Not even magic can make anything bigger than the topmost turret of the palace," he explained. "But now the goblins stand almost as high as your shoulders – when you're human-sized."

Kirsty shivered. "We'll have to be careful," she said solemnly.

Rachel nodded.

"Thank you," said the King gratefully, as the Queen scattered fairy dust over the girls. It whipped up around them, and in a few seconds, a whirlwind was gently lifting them into the sky.

"Goodbye!" Kirsty and Rachel called.

"Rachel's here!" Kirsty shouted, pulling on her boots as the Walkers' car turned into the driveway. It was the day after she and Rachel had been to Fairyland, and Rachel's parents had agreed that Rachel could come and stay. Kirsty had been worried that the Walkers wouldn't be able to make it to Wetherbury, though. The goblins had been up to their tricks overnight and it was snowing heavily.

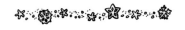

Kirsty dashed outside, followed by her mum and dad.

"Hello," called Mr Tate. "Isn't the weather awful?"

"Come in and have a cup of tea," Mrs Tate offered.

"Lovely," Rachel's mum agreed. "But we mustn't stay long, in case the snow gets worse."

"Come and see Doodle," Kirsty said quietly to Rachel, as their parents chatted.

"Oh, poor Doodle!" said Rachel when she saw the rusty metal. "We must find his feathers, Kirsty!"

A knock at the front door made them both look round. Kirsty's mum opened the door, and greeted an elderly lady.

"It's Mrs Fordham," Kirsty whispered to Rachel. "She lives on Willow Hill."

"I'm sorry to bother you," Mrs Fordham was saying, "but there's so much snow, I can't get home. Could I wait here for a while?"

"Of course," said Mrs Tate, helping her inside. "Come and have a cup of tea."

"I've never seen weather like this," Mrs Fordham went on. "And it seems to be worse on Willow Hill than anywhere else!"

Kirsty and Rachel glanced at each other. "Maybe that's where the goblin is with the Snow Feather!" Kirsty whispered.

"Let's go and find out," Rachel suggested.

Kirsty ran to ask her mum if she and Rachel could play in the snow. Meanwhile, Rachel quickly changed out of her summer clothes. Then the girls said goodbye to their parents, and hurried outside. It was still snowing.

"Quick," said Kirsty. "We must reach Willow Hill before the goblin gets away."

"Wait for me!" called a silvery voice.

Kirsty and Rachel spun round. A tiny fairy was sliding down the drainpipe. She wore a soft blue dress with fluffy white edging.

"It's Crystal the Snow Fairy!" Kirsty gasped.

The girls rushed over to her.

"Hello again!" Crystal called, as tiny, sparkling snowflakes fizzed from the tip of her wand.

"We think your feather is close by," Rachel told her.

"So do I," agreed Crystal. "But there must be a goblin nearby, too, so we have to be careful." She fluttered down and landed on Rachel's shoulder. "Let's go!"

 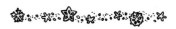
They went out of the Tates' garden, and up Twisty Lane towards the High Street.

Kirsty pointed ahead. "There's Willow Hill," she said breathlessly.

Rachel's heart sank. The snow-covered hill looked very high. As they trudged out of the village, the snow seemed to be getting deeper, too.

"I've got an idea," Kirsty said suddenly, as her feet sank into a snowdrift. "Why don't we use some of our fairy dust? Then we can fly the rest of the way!"

"Good idea!" Crystal said.

Kirsty and Rachel opened their lockets. They each took a pinch of fairy dust and sprinkled it over themselves. Immediately, they began to shrink and their wings grew.

"Let's fly to the top of the hill," Crystal urged. "I can see a house up there."

"That's Willow Cottage," explained Kirsty, "Mrs Fordham's house."

Crystal and the girls flew to the top of the hill, dodging the falling snowflakes. As they neared the cottage, Kirsty spotted smoke coming from the chimney. "That's funny!" she said. "Mrs Fordham lives alone, and she's at our house. So who lit the fire?"

"Let's look inside," suggested Crystal.

They hovered outside a frosty window, while Crystal waved her wand to melt some of the frost and make a spyhole. Then they peered inside.

Sitting on the floor, in front of a roaring fire, was a mean-looking goblin. And in his hand was a shimmering copper feather, speckled with snowy-white.

"It's the Snow Feather!" Crystal gasped.

As the friends watched, the goblin sneezed. "A-TISH-O-O-O!" A shower of ice cubes clattered onto the floor. "The goblin can't use the magic feather properly," Crystal whispered.

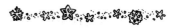

The goblin huddled closer to the fire, rubbing his toes. "My chilblains hurt," he moaned.

Crystal smiled. "Goblins hate to have cold feet!" she murmured.

"How can we get the feather back?" asked Kirsty.

"Let's fly round the house and look for a way in," Rachel suggested.

They flew around, checking all the windows and doors. But everything was locked. They could hear the goblin still muttering about his cold feet.

Kirsty grinned. "I've got an idea!" she said. "Dad's just thrown out a pair of slippers. If I wrap them up in a box, I can deliver the parcel to the goblin. Then he'll open the door."

"Perfect!" Crystal agreed. "The goblin won't be able to resist a present. And if Rachel and I hide inside the box, maybe we can get the feather back."

Quickly, they flew back to the Tates' house. With a touch of her wand, Crystal turned Kirsty human-sized again. Then Kirsty quickly found the slippers, wrapped them in tissue paper and put them in an old shoebox. Crystal and Rachel flew into the shoebox, and hid under the tissue paper. Kirsty popped the lid back on the box and

wrapped it neatly in brown paper. Then she set off again for Willow Hill. She couldn't fly up the hill with the parcel, so she had to walk.

By the time she reached Willow Cottage, she was out of breath and wet with snow. "We're here," she said quietly to Crystal and Rachel. Then she knocked on the door, and waited.

There was no reply.

Kirsty lifted the letter-box. "Delivery!" she called.

"Go away!" the goblin shouted crossly.

Kirsty tried again. "Lovely warm slippers for Mr Goblin!" she said loudly.

This time the door opened, just a crack. Kirsty held the parcel out. The door opened wider, and a bony hand shot out and grabbed the box. Then the door was slammed shut in Kirsty's face.

Kirsty hurried to the window and peeped in. The goblin was tearing the paper off the shoebox. He pulled out the slippers, popped them on his feet and stomped around the room to try them out. They were a bit big, but the goblin settled down happily in front of the fire and fell fast asleep.

 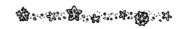

The shining Snow Feather lay on his lap.

Kirsty watched as Crystal and Rachel fluttered out of the shoebox. Crystal flew over to the snoring goblin and lifted the feather up. Then she waved her wand over Rachel, who instantly shot up to her full size.

Rachel opened the window so that she and Crystal could escape, but an icy blast of wind swept into the room.

"What's going on?" the goblin roared, jumping up from his armchair.

"Quick!" Kirsty gasped, pulling Rachel through the window. Crystal zoomed out behind her.

The goblin spotted the Snow Fairy and gave another furious roar. He jumped out of the window and gave chase.

Kirsty and Rachel hurried down the hill. It was hard to run fast because the snow was so deep. "Hurry!" Crystal urged. "He's getting closer!" Rachel glanced anxiously over her shoulder. The goblin was catching up!

But then she saw him trip over in his too-big slippers. Yelling loudly, he rolled head over heels down the hill, picking up snow as he went.

"Watch out, Kirsty!" Rachel gasped. "The goblin's become a giant snowball!"

The goblin's arms and legs stuck out of the snowball as it hurtled down the hill. Quickly, the girls flung themselves out of the way as the snowball shot past them. Soon it was out of sight.

"Are you all right?" asked Crystal, as her friends picked themselves up and brushed snow from their clothes.

"We're fine!" Kirsty beamed. "Can you stop the Snow Feather's magic?"

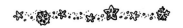 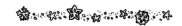

Crystal nodded and waved the
Snow Feather in a complicated pattern.
Immediately, the snow clouds vanished
and the sun shone.

By the time the girls had made their
way back to the Tates' cottage, the
snow had melted away and Mr Tate
had just finished fixing the
weather-vane to the barn roof.

He waved at the girls, and went
to put the ladder away in his shed.

"Quick, Crystal." Kirsty said softly.
"Give Doodle his feather back!"

Crystal nodded, zoomed up to Doodle and slotted
the big tail feather into place.

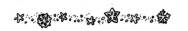 

The girls gasped in surprise as golden sparkles fizzed from Doodle's tail. The iron weather-vane vanished. There in its place was Doodle, as colourful as he had been in Fairyland!

Doodle turned his head, and stared straight at Kirsty and Rachel. "Beware—" he squawked. But before he could say anymore, his feathers began to stiffen and he became metal again.

"What was he trying to say?" Rachel asked.

"I have no idea," Crystal said, shaking her head.

Kirsty frowned. "Maybe he'll tell us more when we return his other feathers."

"Yes," Crystal agreed. She waved at Rachel and Kirsty. "And now I must return to Fairyland. Goodbye and thank you."

"Goodbye!" Rachel and Kirsty called, waving as Crystal flew up into the sky.

"Now we only have six magic feathers to find," Kirsty said.

Rachel nodded. "I wonder where the next one will be!"

Abigail
the Breeze
Fairy

Chapter Two

Abigail the Breeze Fairy

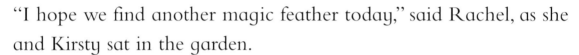

"I hope we find another magic feather today," said Rachel, as she and Kirsty sat in the garden.

The girls knew that the goblins were hiding around Wetherbury, using the magic feathers to conjure up troublesome weather in the village.

Kirsty looked anxious. "We need to find the other feathers," she said. "Or poor Doodle will be stuck on top of our barn forever!"

Just then, Kirsty's mum appeared at the front door. "There you are, Kirsty," she said. "Would you and Rachel like to go to the village fête and give your gran some support in the Cake Competition?"

Kirsty and Rachel looked at each other. "We'd love to," Kirsty replied.

"Well, you'd better hurry if you want to get there before the judging starts," Mrs Tate warned.

A few minutes later, the girls were hurrying down Twisty Lane towards the High Street. As they drew near to a thatched cottage with a pretty garden full of roses, a gust of wind blew a shower of petals onto the pavement.

Then, a large white envelope landed at Kirsty's feet. "Where did that come from?" she murmured, and gasped as more letters came spinning towards her.

"The wind's really picked up," Rachel commented.

"Hey! Come back!" called a voice. A postman was running towards them, chasing the envelopes that had been caught by the breeze.

The girls picked up the letters and handed them to the postman, who stuffed them into his sack.

"Thanks," he grinned. "This wind's blowing something fierce."

He went off to deliver his letters as Kirsty and Rachel hurried on towards the fête.

The wind seemed to be getting stronger and when they arrived at the fête, they saw that it was causing havoc.

Strings of bunting had come loose and were blowing in the wind like kite-tails. Three marquees strained against their guy-ropes as they billowed and swayed. And several stallholders were fighting to stop their goods blowing away.

As the girls set off in search of the Cake Competition, Kirsty noticed a small boy struggling to hold on to a yellow balloon. Suddenly, the wind whipped it out of his hand and sent it

bobbing away across the grass.

"My balloon!" sobbed the boy.

"We'll catch it!" called Kirsty, already giving chase.

Rachel ran after her friend. "There's something very strange about this wind!" she shouted.

"I know," puffed Kirsty, jumping for the balloon's string. "Do you think it could be magic?"

Rachel nodded. And the girls looked at each other, their eyes shining with excitement.

Kirsty and Rachel caught the balloon and took it back to its owner. The boy's face lit up. "Thank you!" he beamed.

"You're welcome," Kirsty replied.

Just then she heard a familiar voice. "Hello, Kirsty," called a jolly-looking lady, bustling over to the girls.

"Hi, Gran," Kirsty said. She turned to Rachel. "This is Grandma Tate," she explained.

"Hello, Mrs Tate," said Rachel. She glanced at the huge cake tin that Kirsty's gran was holding. "Is that your entry for the competition?"

Kirsty's gran nodded. "That grumpy Mrs Adelstrop always wins. But I think I'm in with a chance this year."

"Who's Mrs Adelstrop?" Rachel inquired.

Just then, another woman with a cake tin pushed rudely past. "Out of my way!" she demanded. "This wind is dreadful!"

And with that she disappeared inside the marquee.

"I expect you've guessed who that was," whispered Kirsty's gran.

"Mrs Adelstrop!" chorused the girls.

"Right first time," said Gran with a laugh. "Well, I must dash." And she followed Mrs Adelstrop into the tent.

"Shall we go inside, too?" Kirsty suggested. "The goblin with the Breeze Feather might be hiding in there."

Rachel nodded and the girls wandered into the marquee, just in time to see Mrs Adelstrop smiling confidently as she placed an enormous lemon cake on the table.

"That looks good," Kirsty whispered.

Kirsty's gran took out her chocolate fudge gateau. Layers of chocolate sponge and butter-cream filling were topped with icing and chocolate leaves.

"Wow! That's Gran's best cake ever!" Kirsty exclaimed.

"It looks delicious," Rachel agreed.

But as Mrs Tate stepped forwards to place her cake on the table, a ferocious gust of wind blew into the marquee. A length of coloured bunting snaked into the tent and tangled itself around her legs.

Mrs Tate stumbled and the cake flew out of her hands. It sailed through the air and landed – right in the judge's face!

Kirsty's gran looked horrified. "Oh, how dreadful!" she whispered to the girls.

"What an awful accident," said Mrs Adelstrop loudly. Kirsty thought she was trying not to look pleased.

The judge stood there, covered in chocolate and icing, as everyone rushed to help him clean up.

"The wind's getting worse," whispered Rachel. "See if the goblin is hiding under the table."

Kirsty lifted a corner of the tablecloth and peeped underneath, but there was no sign of a goblin.

Rachel glanced around, looking for other goblin hiding places. Her eyes fell on a pretty fairy decoration on top of a cake. Suddenly, she gasped. The tiny fairy was giving her a cheeky wave!

The fairy's eyes sparkled with laughter. She wore a pretty yellow top and a matching skirt. Her hair was windswept and she held an emerald green wand with coppery leaves swirling from the tip.

"Kirsty! Over here!" Rachel whispered. Kirsty hurried over. "It's Abigail the Breeze Fairy."

"Hello, girls!" Abigail said.

"We think there's a goblin nearby," Rachel told her.

Abigail's face paled. "Goblins are nasty things but we have to find this one," she said bravely, "before he does any more mischief with the Breeze Feather."

"Well, the goblin isn't in here," said Kirsty. "Let's go outside."

"Good idea," Rachel agreed, and the two friends left the marquee, struggling to make headway against the wind.

They hadn't got far when there was a loud creaking noise, and suddenly the marquee collapsed! The girls saw Kirsty's gran rushing to help others who were crawling out from the canvas.

"Oh, what a mess!" said Rachel. "But at least it doesn't look as if anyone's hurt."

"This is more goblin mischief!" fumed Kirsty. "If he keeps using the Breeze Feather, he'll ruin the fête."

Quickly, the girls searched the tents and some of the stalls for the goblin.

Then, Kirsty noticed a dog barking. "It's Twiglet," she said, pointing at an adorable Jack Russell puppy beside the Tombola. "His owner is Mr McDougall."

"We haven't searched the Tombola yet," Rachel said. "Let's check for goblins."

The girls hurried over. "Hello," Kirsty said.

"Hello, lass," said Mr McDougall. "I reckon Twiglet doesn't like this windstorm."

Kirsty nodded. She bent down to stroke Twiglet and the puppy jumped up from beside his empty bowl, wagging his tail.

"What's that?" Rachel asked, pointing to a torn piece of material in Twiglet's mouth.

Kirsty coaxed the material away from Twiglet. It was brownish leather and it smelled mouldy.

"I'm sure I've seen something like it before," Rachel said thoughtfully. "I wonder where it came from."

Suddenly, Twiglet began barking again. He was staring up at the sky.

"That's odd," said Mr McDougall. "He keeps doing that."

"Maybe he's hungry?" suggested Rachel.

"Can't be," Mr McDougall replied. "His dish is empty. He must have bolted his food when I wasn't looking."

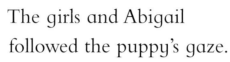

Twiglet growled crossly, still looking upwards. The girls and Abigail followed the puppy's gaze.

"Look at that!" Rachel said, pointing to a hot-air balloon floating above the fête.

The fierce wind sent leaves and bits of paper whirling around it, but the balloon itself seemed to hang almost stationary in mid-air.

"That's odd," said Kirsty. "It doesn't seem to be affected by the wind at all!"

Abigail gave an excited cry. "The goblin must be hiding in it!" she exclaimed. "Only the magic Breeze Feather could protect the balloon from the wind like that."

Kirsty's eyes widened. "We've found the goblin," she said. "But he's way up in the sky!"

"How are we going to get up there?" Rachel asked.

"Easy!" Abigail told her. "We use fairy magic!"

The girls immediately reached for their shining golden lockets full of fairy dust.

They sprinkled themselves with the magic dust and laughed in delight as they shrank to become fairies.

"We must hurry!" Abigail said, zooming into the air, quickly followed by Kirsty and Rachel.

The higher Abigail and the girls flew, the more the wind tore at them and tried to blow them off course. Kirsty and Rachel soon felt their wings tiring.

"Fly in my path," Abigail urged. "You'll find it easier."

Rachel and Kirsty did as she said and gradually they drew nearer to the balloon's basket.

"We were right. Look!" gasped Kirsty.

An ugly face peered over the edge of the basket. It was a goblin with pointed ears and a lumpy nose. The goblin was staring at Twiglet, who was still barking down below.

"Silly little doggy. You can't catch me!" he sneered.

Kirsty and Rachel heard the goblin's tummy rumble. It sounded like mud being stirred in a bucket. The goblin gave a huge burp and a blast of stinky breath gusted over the friends.

"Yuk!" complained Rachel. "Whatever has that goblin been eating?"

"Can't catch me, doggy!" taunted the goblin, and he waved a shining bronze feather. Immediately, a strong gust of wind swept Twiglet off his feet. The puppy tumbled over, got up again, and began barking even more loudly.

The goblin jumped back, looking a little alarmed. Then he recovered. "I'm safe up here!" he said to himself, and laughed.

Rachel felt puzzled. *The goblin's afraid of Twiglet*, she thought. *I wonder why*?

"He's holding the Breeze Feather!" snapped Abigail.

"Yes. And he's using it to tease poor Twiglet!" said Kirsty. "What a cheek!"

"I've got a plan," Rachel told her friends. "Kirsty, you land in the basket. Then Abigail can make you big and the two of you can distract the goblin while I fly up and turn off the balloon's burner. The balloon will sink, and we'll have a better chance of getting the feather back once the goblin's grounded."

"It's a good idea," said Abigail. "But Kirsty and I will be very close to the goblin. Can you be quick, Rachel?"

Rachel nodded.

"Here I go," Kirsty said, fluttering up and over the lip of the basket.

Abigail hovered next to her. With a wave of her wand, she turned Kirsty back to her normal size.

The goblin's eyes bulged as big as golf balls when he saw Kirsty. "Who are you?" he demanded.

"I'm Kirsty, a friend of the Weather Fairies," Kirsty declared firmly.

"And I'm Abigail the Breeze Fairy," Abigail added.

"Boo!" the goblin shouted, and lunged at Abigail.

She fluttered away in alarm and the goblin snorted with laughter

Behind the goblin's back, Kirsty saw Rachel turning off the burner.

The goblin turned and scowled at Kirsty. "Get off my balloon!" he roared.

"That's not very polite," Kirsty said calmly.

"Don't care!" snapped the goblin. He looked at Abigail slyly. "I know what you want and you shan't have it!" he said, waving the Breeze Feather.

A huge gust of wind rocked the basket. Kirsty clung to the side as it tipped dangerously.

The goblin sniggered. "Too windy for you, is it?"

"Your balloon's sinking," Kirsty told him.

"Codswallop!" sneered the goblin. Then he looked over the edge of the basket. "Oo-er!"

Below them, but getting nearer all the time, Twiglet barked and growled. The goblin's big nose twitched nervously.

Kirsty noticed a big rip in his leathery robe and remembered the piece of material in Twiglet's mouth. "Why are you afraid of the puppy?" she asked.

The goblin looked shifty. "I *might* have eaten his dinner," he replied sulkily.

No wonder his breath is so stinky! thought Kirsty.

"Now, tell me why this balloon's sinking!" demanded the goblin. "Or I'll wave the Breeze Feather and tip you out – like this!"

The basket rocked back and forth. Kirsty's heart pounded, but she clung on to the side. The goblin hardly moved; he was perfectly balanced on his big broad feet.

Kirsty reached anxiously for her fairy locket. Would she have time to use the fairy dust if she fell?

"There's too much weight on board! That's why we're sinking," said Abigail.

The goblin glared at Kirsty. "You're too heavy. Get out!" he ordered.

Quick as a flash, Kirsty sprinkled herself with fairy dust from her locket and fluttered out of the goblin's way.

"We're still sinking!" the goblin exclaimed in alarm. "What shall I do?"

Abigail put her hands on her hips. "You'll have to throw out that feather!" she told the goblin firmly.

"Shan't!" snapped the goblin. "It's mine! Besides, it's too light to make any difference."

Kirsty and Rachel hovered behind Abigail.

"It's a lot heavier than you think," Abigail said craftily.

The goblin scowled. "What do you mean?"

"A kilo of feathers weighs just the same as a kilo of rocks, you know," she replied.

Kirsty and Rachel laughed softly. They knew that a kilo of anything weighs just the same as a kilo of anything else! But goblins are foolish, and the girls guessed that Abigail was hoping to confuse this one. The goblin blinked and scratched his head. On the ground below, Twiglet barked and jumped up at the balloon. He seemed a lot closer now.

"Argh! Don't let it get me!" screamed the goblin, flinging the feather out of the basket. Abigail shot after it in a blur of golden wings, but the feather was caught by the wind and swept away.

"Come on!" shouted Rachel, flying after Abigail. Kirsty followed. "The wind's too strong. I can't fly!" cried Rachel in panic.

The girls were tossed and tumbled around by the wind. They flapped their wings and tried to regain control, but it was no use. They were drifting further from the Breeze Feather, and they couldn't even see Abigail.

"We have to reach the feather," shouted Kirsty. "Otherwise it could be lost for ever!"

Suddenly, Kirsty and Rachel caught sight of Abigail flying to their rescue.

"Don't worry about us," Kirsty shouted.

"Just catch the Breeze Feather!" Rachel yelled.

Abigail must have heard them because she nodded firmly and sped off. She was about to grab the feather when the wind snatched it away from her. Rachel let out a cry of despair, but then she saw a rope of tiny golden leaves snake out from Abigail's wand and wrap around the Breeze Feather.

The tiny fairy pulled the feather towards her and finally managed to catch hold of it. She immediately waved it in a complicated pattern. "Wind, stop!" she ordered. With a soft sigh, the roaring wind died.

Kirsty and Rachel immediately found that they could fly properly again.

Abigail flew to join them. "It's wonderful to have the Breeze Feather back safely!" she said happily.

"What about the goblin?" asked Kirsty.

Abigail frowned. "Leave him to me!" She pointed the feather at the hot-air balloon.

"Wind, blow!" she commanded. An enormous puff of wind rocked the balloon.

The goblin hung over the basket. His face looked greenish. "I feel sick," he moaned.

"You shouldn't have eaten Twiglet's dinner!" Rachel told him.

"I wish I hadn't now," replied the goblin gloomily.

Abigail waved the Breeze Feather a second time and the balloon was blown high into the sky and out of sight.

Kirsty, Rachel, and Abigail fluttered down to the fête and slid down the roof of one of the tents to the ground.

Abigail waved her wand and Kirsty and Rachel grew to normal size.

They peeped out from behind the tent. People were rushing about setting their stalls to rights, and over at the Tombola, Twiglet was chewing contentedly.

"Mr McDougall has given Twiglet a chewstick," said Kirsty.

"I bet it tastes better than goblin's clothes!" laughed Rachel.

"Kirsty!" called Kirsty's gran.

Abigail quickly zoomed onto Kirsty's shoulder and hid beneath her hair.

"Gran!" Suddenly Kirsty remembered what had happened to her gran's cake. So why was her gran wearing such a broad grin.

"I won first prize!" said Mrs Tate, her eyes shining. "The judge said my cake was delicious. He couldn't help tasting it when it was all over his face!"

The girls were just congratulating Mrs Tate when Mrs Adelstrop stomped past, scowling.

Kirsty's gran chuckled. "Must go," she said. "My best friend, Mable, is hoping to win a prize in one of the vegetable competitions!"

Kirsty and Rachel waved goodbye.

"We should go and give Doodle his magic feather back," said Kirsty.

The girls and Abigail headed home.

Back at Kirsty's house, Abigail flew straight up to the barn roof and carefully put the Breeze Feather into Doodle's tail.

The weather-vane cockerel fizzed into life and shook himself.

Fabulous copper sparkles flew into the air, making Rachel and Kirsty gasp in wonder. Doodle's fiery feathers were magnificent.

Doodle shifted to settle the Breeze Feather properly into place. Then he looked straight at Rachel and Kirsty.

"Jack—" he squawked, and opened his beak as if to speak again, but the colour ebbed from his feathers. Doodle became a rusty old weather-vane once more.

"He's trying to tell us something," said Kirsty.

"Last time, he said 'Beware'," Rachel reminded Kirsty. "So now we have 'Beware Jack…' I wonder what he wanted to say next?"

Abigail floated down from the roof. "I don't know," she said. "But keep your eyes open. Jack Frost is always up to mischief."

"We will," Kirsty promised.

"Now I must fly back to Fairyland," Abigail said. "Thank you girls."

"Goodbye, Abigail!" Kirsty said, and Rachel waved.

Abigail's wings flashed, and with a swirl of tiny golden leaves, she was gone.

Rachel and Kirsty smiled at each other.

"Five more magic feathers to find!" whispered Kirsty.

Pearl
the Cloud
Fairy

Chapter Three

Pearl the Cloud Fairy

"What's the weather like, Kirsty?" asked Rachel eagerly. She pushed back the duvet. "Do you think there's magic in the air?"

Kirsty was standing at the bedroom window. "It seems like an ordinary day," she sighed. "The sky's cloudy."

"Never mind." Rachel jumped out of bed to join her friend. She pointed at the weather-vane on top of the barn. "Look at Doodle. Don't you think he looks a bit happier now that he's got two tail feathers back?"

Kirsty nodded. "Let's hope we find all his feathers before you go home," she replied.

"Girls, are you awake?" Kirsty's mum called from downstairs. "Breakfast's ready."

"Coming," Kirsty shouted back.

The girls got dressed quickly and clattered downstairs.

"Morning, you two," said Mr Tate as the girls sat down. "What are you planning to do today?"

Before Kirsty or Rachel could answer him, there was a knock at the back door.

"I wonder who that can be!" Mrs Tate said, raising her eyebrows. "It's still quite early."

"I'll get it," said Kirsty. She opened the door. Outside stood Mr and Mrs Twitching, the Tates' elderly neighbours.

"Good morning, Kirsty," said Mr Twitching. "We're sorry to disturb you, but have you seen Fidget?"

Kirsty knew Fidget, the Twitchings' fluffy tabby cat, very well, but she hadn't seen her for the last day or two. "I'm afraid I haven't recently," she replied.

"Oh, dear," Mrs Twitching said, looking upset. "She didn't come home for her dinner last night."

"Come in and ask Mum and Dad," Kirsty suggested. "Perhaps they've seen her."

As Mr and Mrs Twitching walked into the kitchen, Kirsty blinked. Just for a moment she'd thought she'd seen strange wisps of smoke drifting over the neighbours' heads. She glanced at Rachel and her parents, but they didn't seem to have noticed anything unusual. Kirsty shook her head. Maybe she was imagining it…

"When did you last see Fidget?" asked Kirsty's mum.

"Yesterday afternoon," Mrs Twitching replied. "She doesn't usually miss a single meal."

"Kirsty and I could help you look for her," suggested Rachel.

"Good idea," Kirsty agreed, finishing off her cereal. "Let's go right away."

"And I'll check our garden," added Mr Tate.

As Kirsty and Rachel got up from the table, Kirsty stared extra-hard at the Twitchings' heads. She thought she could see wisps of smoke hovering there again, but it was difficult to be sure.

"Rachel," Kirsty said quietly, after the neighbours had gone, "did you notice anything funny about the Twitchings?"

52

Rachel looked puzzled. "What do you mean?" Kirsty explained about the wisps of smoke. "Do you think they could have been magic?" Rachel asked curiously. Kirsty felt a thrill of excitement. "Maybe," she said. "We'd better keep our eyes open for magic as well as Fidget!" The girls walked into the village, keeping a sharp look-out for the tabby cat, but there was no sign of her.

"I hope Fidget isn't lost for good," Kirsty said anxiously, staring around. "Oh!" Kirsty hadn't been looking where she was going, and she'd bumped into one of the villagers. "I'm so sorry," she said politely.

The woman glared at her. "Be more careful!" she snapped, and hurried off.

"Well!" gasped Rachel. "That wasn't very nice."

But Kirsty was looking puzzled. "That was Mrs Hill, one of my mum's friends, and she's usually lovely," she replied. "I wonder what's wrong?"

The girls wandered into the park. "Everybody's in a miserable mood," Rachel whispered. "Look at the children."

Kirsty stared at the children in the playground. They didn't seem to be enjoying their games at all. Every single one of them looked sad and sulky.

"I think we've been all round Wetherbury. And there's no sign of Fidget anywhere," Kirsty sighed, glancing at her watch. "We'd better go home."

Rachel nodded. "We can always carry on searching later."

The girls turned back towards the Tates' house. On the way they passed the tiny village cinema. The Saturday morning show had just finished, and the audience was flooding out. Just like everyone else, the people looked glum.

"It must have been a sad film," Rachel whispered to Kirsty.

"But it wasn't," Kirsty replied, frowning. "Look." She pointed at the poster outside the cinema.

"*This hilarious film is a must! You'll split your sides laughing!*" Rachel read. "Well, the audience definitely didn't find it funny," Rachel pointed out. "Look at their faces."

Kirsty stared at the people and suddenly her heart began to pound. She could definitely see cloudy smoke drifting over the cinema-goers' heads. "Look, Rachel!" She nudged her friend. "There's that smoke again."

Rachel peered at the people. For a moment she thought Kirsty was seeing things. But then she spotted the clouds of smoke too. "It must be fairy magic!" Rachel said excitedly.

"Yes," Kirsty agreed. "We could be on the trail of another magic feather!"

The girls hurried home. When they entered the house, the first thing they noticed were the clouds hovering over Mr and Mrs Tate!

"Did you find Fidget?" asked Kirsty's mum, who was sitting on the sofa, reading a book. The little white cloud above her head was touched with pink, like a sunset cloud.

"No," Kirsty replied, staring at the grey cloud which was over her dad.

55

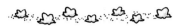

"Oh, dear," Mr Tate said, looking sad.

"I think the goblin with the magic Cloud Feather is close by," Rachel whispered to Kirsty as they ate their sandwiches.

Kirsty nodded. "After lunch, let's go up to my bedroom and plan our next move," she said. "These clouds are beginning to worry me."

"Me, too," Rachel agreed.

As soon as they'd finished their food, the girls ran upstairs. Kirsty threw open her bedroom door.

"Hello!" called a silvery voice. "I thought you were never coming!" There, on the windowsill, sat Pearl the Cloud Fairy.

Pearl was resting her chin on her hands, and she too looked fed up. She wore a beautiful pink and white dress and, in her hand, she held a pretty pink wand from which little pink and white clouds constantly drifted.

A tiny grey cloud hovered over Pearl's head. "Oh, Pearl! You've got a raincloud, too!" Kirsty burst out.

"I know," Pearl sighed. "It's because a nasty goblin is using the magic Cloud Feather – and he's doing it all wrong!" she snapped.

"We think the goblin must be very nearby. Everyone in Wetherbury seems to have a cloud over them," Rachel told Pearl.

"I'm sure you're right," Pearl said firmly. "Even you two are beginning to get clouds now!"

The girls rushed over to the mirror to look. Sure enough, tiny wisps of smoke were beginning to form above their heads.

"Shall we go and find the Cloud Feather?" Kirsty asked eagerly.

Pearl and Rachel both cheered up at that suggestion. Pearl zoomed over to hide herself in Rachel's jacket pocket. Then they all went out into the village.

This time, Rachel and Kirsty could see the clouds over people's heads much more clearly. Some were a pretty pink like sunset clouds, and the people underneath seemed quiet and dreamy. Other clouds were black and stormy and the people under those looked gloomy and irritable.

"Pearl," Kirsty whispered. "Why hasn't anyone else noticed the clouds?"

Pearl popped her head out of Rachel's pocket. "Only magic beings like fairies can see them," she replied. "And you two, because you're our friends."

"They're getting bigger," said Rachel, staring at a woman with an enormous raincloud above her head.

"We must be getting closer to the feather!" Pearl said.

"But where can it be?" Kirsty wondered. She stopped and looked around. Suddenly she gasped, and pointed at a building to their left. "Look at the sweet factory!"

The sweet factory stood right on the edge of Wetherbury, and small pink and white clouds were streaming from its tall chimney.

"The goblin must be hiding in there," Pearl cried. "It's time to rescue the Cloud Feather!"

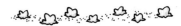

The girls and Pearl rushed over to the door. But their hearts sank when they saw the heavy padlock.

"It's Saturday. The factory's closed," Kirsty said. "What shall we do?"

They stood and thought for a moment. Then Rachel glanced up and smiled. "Look!" she said, pointing. "There's an air vent near the roof. Let's turn ourselves into fairies with the magic dust. Then we can all fly in through the vent."

"Good idea!" Pearl laughed.

Quickly, Rachel and Kirsty opened their lockets, and sprinkled a little fairy dust over themselves. Immediately, they began to shrink, and shimmering fairy wings appeared on their backs.

"Up we go!" Pearl cried, whizzing up to the air vent in the wall. She slipped through and the two girls followed. They all stopped just inside, and gazed around the factory.

"Wow!" Kirsty breathed.

Lots of big machines were busy making all sorts of different sweets. Stripy humbugs poured from one.

Long strings of strawberry liquorice were piped out of another. Bright yellow sherbert fizzed into paper tubes, and pink and white marshmallows bounced along a conveyor-belt. Chocolate bars were being wrapped in gold foil, while a different machine wrapped toffees in shiny silver paper.

Kirsty looked puzzled. "But nobody's working today, so who turned all the machines on?" she asked.

"The goblin!" Pearl exclaimed. "Let's split up, and see if we can spot him."

They fluttered off to different parts of the factory. Rachel flew towards a machine which was hard at work mixing candyfloss. She hovered over the machine for a moment and was about to fly on, when she heard the sound of someone loudly smacking their lips.

Rachel flew down to take a closer look. There, lying on a huge, fluffy cloud and greedily munching candyfloss was the

60

goblin. He was quite big and round – probably from stuffing himself with candyfloss, Rachel thought.

She flew a little nearer to see if she could spy the magic Cloud Feather. There it was – pearly-grey and shimmering in his hand. Tiny pink and white clouds drifted from it, as the goblin waved it about.

I must tell Pearl and Kirsty, Rachel thought. She turned to fly off, but as she did so, one wing brushed the goblin's shoulder.

With a roar of surprise, the goblin reached up and grabbed Rachel tightly. "You're not having my feather!" he shouted, and stuffed Rachel inside a pink cloud which was drifting past.

Poor Rachel was trapped. She tried to push her way out of the cloud, but she couldn't make a hole in it. The cloud drifted up and away from the goblin.

"Kirsty! Pearl!" Rachel called as loudly as she could. "HELP!"

Kirsty heard her friend's voice. She turned, and saw the cloud with Rachel inside it. To Kirsty's horror, it was heading straight towards the factory's chimney.

"Oh, no!" Kirsty gasped. "If that cloud floats up the chimney, we'll never get Rachel back!"

Pearl flew over to join Kirsty. "Don't worry, I'll get Rachel's cloud," she said.

"That goblin!" Kirsty exclaimed crossly. "I've got a few things to say to him! Can you make me human-sized again?"

Pearl nodded. "I'll find Rachel. You get the feather," she said, and with a wave of her wand, he turned Kirsty back to her normal size. Then she flew off to search the clouds. Kirsty stormed angrily over to the goblin, who was lying on his fluffy cloud, still eating candyfloss. When he saw Kirsty marching towards him, he looked nervous. Quickly, he stuffed the Cloud Feather into his mouth out of sight.

"Give me that feather!" Kirsty demanded.

"Wha' fe'er?" the goblin spluttered, trying to keep his mouth closed.

Kirsty frowned. How was she going to get the feather out of the goblin's mouth? She spotted a candyfloss stick lying on the floor. That gave her an idea. She picked it up, and began tickling the goblin on the soles of his leathery feet!

The goblin began to chuckle. "Shtop it," he mumbled. But then he couldn't hold his laughter in any longer. "Oh, ha ha ha," he guffawed. And as his laughter burst out, so did the magic Cloud Feather!

Kirsty made a grab for it, but the goblin was quicker. "Oh, no!" he grinned, catching the feather. "This is *my* feather! I'm the only one who knows how to make it work."

"Actually, I do too!" called a silvery voice.

Kirsty turned to see Pearl flying towards them, towing a pink cloud behind her with Rachel inside.

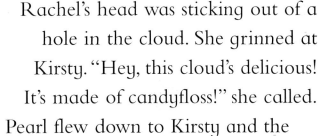

Rachel's head was sticking out of a hole in the cloud. She grinned at Kirsty. "Hey, this cloud's delicious! It's made of candyfloss!" she called. Pearl flew down to Kirsty and the goblin. "I can make the clouds do anything," she went on. "I can even make them dance around me." She held out her hand to the goblin. "Give me the feather and let me show you!"

The goblin looked sly. "No, it's mine!" he said. "Anyway, I can do that myself."

"Go on, then," Pearl challenged.

The goblin frowned in concentration and waved the feather. Very slowly, all the clouds in the room drifted towards him.

He twiddled the feather, and the clouds began to whirl around him in a circle, faster and faster. "See?" the goblin boasted.

"OK, you know what to do, Rachel," Pearl whispered to her.

Pearl let go of Rachel's candyfloss cloud and it sailed over to the goblin. Then it began to whizz around him along with the others.

Suddenly, just as her cloud sped past the goblin's hand, Rachel stuck her arm out of the hole and seized the Cloud Feather!

"Give that back!" the goblin shouted. Every time Rachel's cloud flew past him, he tried to grab the feather, but missed.

The clouds were whizzing round so fast now that Rachel was feeling dizzy. "Help!" she called. "Somebody stop this cloud!"

Pearl swooped down and deftly plucked the feather out of Rachel's hand. Then she waved it expertly a few times, and the clouds began to slow down and drift away.

Kirsty caught hold of Rachel's cloud, and pulled it open to free her friend. Rachel tumbled out, dizzily. The goblin was dizzy too, from all the clouds whirling round his head.

He was staggering around in circles, looking for the Cloud Feather. When he saw that Pearl had it, he lurched forward and made a clumsy grab for the little fairy.

Pearl darted out of the way just in time, but the goblin lost his balance. He tumbled over, and fell head-first into the toffee-wrapping machine!

The girls and Pearl watched in amazement as the yelling goblin was wrapped in a huge sheet of shiny silver paper. Then the goblin-shaped toffee was shunted along the conveyor-belt, boxed and gift-wrapped with a sparkly silver ribbon.

"That serves him right!" Rachel laughed.

"Come on," grinned Pearl. "Let's get out of here before he unwraps himself!"

Kirsty sprinkled herself with fairy dust and immediately turned into a fairy again. Then the three friends flew out of the factory through the air vent. Outside, Pearl waved her magic wand and returned the girls to normal. "And I'd better make sure everyone in Wetherbury gets back to normal right away!" Pearl laughed. She waved the feather again. "That should do it," she declared cheerfully.

They set off back to Kirsty's house, with Pearl hiding in Rachel's pocket.

"Look," whispered Rachel, as they made their way through the village. "No one has a cloud over their head anymore!"

"And everyone's happy and laughing again," added Kirsty.

"I'll give Doodle his beautiful Cloud Feather back," Pearl said, when they arrived at the Tates' house.

Rachel and Kirsty watched happily as Pearl replaced the Cloud Feather in Doodle's tail. A moment later, the cockerel's fiery feathers began to sparkle with fairy magic.

"Doodle's coming to life again!" Kirsty cried. "Listen hard, Rachel!"

Doodle's magnificent feathers shimmered in the sun. "Frost w—!" he squawked. But the next moment, he was cold, hard metal again.

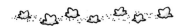

"Beware, Jack Frost w—" Kirsty said thoughtfully, as Pearl flew down to join them. "What does it mean?"

"I don't know," replied Pearl. "But be careful, girls!" The pretty fairy hugged Rachel and Kirsty, scattering little pink clouds around them. Then she fluttered up into the sky. "Now I must go home. Goodbye!" she called.

"Goodbye!" replied Kirsty and Rachel.

Smiling, Pearl waved her wand and disappeared into the clouds. The girls went into the house.

"Oh, Kirsty, Rachel, here you are at last," said Mrs Tate. "The

Twitchings phoned and invited us over for tea."

"And they said they've got some good news for us," Mr Tate added.

Kirsty and Rachel looked at each other. "They must have found Fidget!" Kirsty guessed.

The girls hurried next-door with Mr and Mrs Tate.

Mr Twitching opened the door, a big smile on his face. "Come in," he said.

He led them into the living-room, where Mrs Twitching was kneeling on the rug next to a cat basket. A big, fluffy tabby cat was curled up inside.

"She's been a very busy girl," Mrs Twitching said proudly. "Look!" There in the basket were three tiny kittens, snuggled up to their mum. Two were tabby like Fidget, and one was black with a little white spot on top of its head.

"Oh, Rachel, aren't they gorgeous?" Kirsty breathed, stroking the black and white kitten on its tiny head.

"We'll be looking for good homes for them when they're bigger," said Mr Twitching. "But they can't leave their mum for eight or nine weeks."

"Oh!" Kirsty gasped, her eyes shining. "Maybe I could have one?"

"I don't see why not," Mrs Tate said, smiling.

"Which one would you like, Kirsty?" Mrs Twitching asked.

"This one," Kirsty said, stroking the black and white kitten again. It yawned sleepily.

"And I know the perfect name for her," Rachel said, smiling at her friend. "You can call her Pearl!"

Goldie
the Sunshine Fairy

Chapter Four

Goldie the Sunshine Fairy

"I feel as if I'm about to melt," said Rachel happily.

It was a hot summer afternoon and she and Kirsty were enjoying the sunshine. A bumblebee buzzed lazily around Mrs Tate's sunflowers, and a single breath of wind whispered through the rose bushes.

The weather had been so warm, Mr and Mrs Tate had given the girls permission to camp out in the garden overnight.

Kirsty looked up from a jumble of tent poles. "It's been a perfect day," she agreed. "Let's hope tonight is perfect, too. I don't fancy lying out here in the rain, do you?"

Rachel laughed. "I think I'd rather have a shower in the morning, not in the middle of the night," she agreed.

Kirsty held up some poles. "How do we put this thing together, then?" she asked brightly.

Rachel scratched her head. "Well..."

"Need some help?" came a voice from behind them.

"Dad!" said Kirsty in relief. "Yes, please. We—" She burst out laughing as she looked at her father. Rachel turned to see what was so funny and had to bite her lip not to laugh, too. For there, standing in front of them, was Mr Tate, wearing the most enormous sunglasses she had ever seen.

Mr Tate was looking pleased. "Do you like my new shades?" he asked.

"Well, yes," Kirsty said, trying to keep a straight face. "They're very...summery."

Mr Tate knelt down and started putting the tent together. "The weather has been strange recently," he said. "I hope it doesn't start snowing again!"

Rachel and Kirsty looked at each other but didn't say anything. They knew *exactly* why the weather had been so strange.

Yesterday, with the help of Pearl the Cloud Fairy, Kirsty and Rachel had returned the Cloud Feather to Doodle. But there were still four magic weather feathers left to find.

"There!" said Mr Tate, admiring the finished tent. "It's all yours."

"Thanks, Dad," Kirsty said as he walked away. She flopped down on the grass. "Phew!" she whistled. "It's still so hot!"

Rachel was frowning and looking at her watch. "Kirsty," she said slowly. "Have you noticed where the sun is?"

Kirsty looked up and pointed. "Right there, in the sky," she replied helpfully.

"Yes, but look how high it is," Rachel insisted. "It hasn't even *started* setting yet."

Kirsty glanced at her watch. "But it's half-past seven," she said. Now she was frowning, too. "So that can't be right."

Rachel had just opened her mouth to reply, when there was a loud *Pop!* "What was that?" she whispered.

Pop! Pop! Pop!

"It sounds like it's coming from the other side of the hedge," Kirsty answered. "But there's only a cornfield over there."

Curiously, the girls peeped over the hedge to see what was making all the noise.

"I don't believe it," Kirsty said, rubbing her eyes. "Is that what I think it is?"

Pop! Pop! Pop!

Rachel nodded. "Popcorn," she breathed.

It was an amazing sight. The sun was so hot that the corn in the field was literally cooking – and turning into popcorn! Both girls stared as golden puffs of corn bounced everywhere, as if the field was one enormous saucepan. A delicious smell of popcorn drifted over the hedge.

"There's definitely magic in the air," Kirsty said.

"It must be the goblin with the Sunshine Feather," Rachel agreed.

Both girls peered hard at the field, hoping to spot a goblin lurking somewhere, but it was difficult to see clearly through the popcorn tumbling and twirling in the sky.

Rachel suddenly grabbed Kirsty's hand. "Look!" she cried.

Kirsty stared. Darting above the corn was a twinkling yellow light. It was zigzagging through the air between the flying pieces of popcorn and heading straight towards them. As it came closer, the air above the field seemed to glitter with a thousand tiny sparkles. Both girls could see a pair of delicate golden wings beating quickly, and the glimmer of a tiny wand.

"It's Goldie the Sunshine Fairy," whispered Rachel in delight.

The fairy weaved in and out of the bouncing corn, neatly dodging each piece. Then she swooped down to land on the hedge near the girls. "Wow!" she laughed. "Talk about a bumpy ride!"

Kirsty and Rachel watched as Goldie shook popcorn dust from her glittering wings. Her face was framed by long, curly, blonde hair, and she wore a gauzy dress in fiery reds, yellows and oranges.

"Hello again," said Goldie. "I've been hearing how you've helped Crystal, Abigail and Pearl. You've done brilliantly!" Rachel and Kirsty grinned at each other proudly.

"The goblin who has the Sunshine Feather can't be far away," Goldie went on, looking up at the sky where the sun was still blazing brightly.

"That's what we thought," Kirsty said. "There's a farm on the other side of this field. Shall we start looking there?"

"Good idea," Goldie replied cheerfully. But her face fell as she looked at the cornfield where popcorn was still whizzing around. "Is there another way across the field, though?"

Goldie sighed. "I don't fancy dodging that popcorn again," she said.

"There's a lane that runs down the side of the field to the farm," Kirsty told her. "We'll ask Mum if we can go for a quick walk before bedtime."

Minutes later, the three of them were on their way. The air was practically shimmering with heat and there were cracks in the ground where the earth had become hardened by the sun.

Once they reached the farm, the girls and Goldie started searching for the goblin. First they peeped into the stables, where two very hot-looking horses were sheltering from the sun.

"Hello," Goldie said. "Have you seen a goblin hanging around?"

One of the horses shook her mane. "All we've seen is this stable," she said. "And there are no goblins in here."

"It's too hot to go out," the other horse whinnied.

Next, the girls and Goldie slipped into the cowshed. The cows were all half-asleep in the heat, and quite grumpy at being disturbed. There was no goblin.

At last the three friends came to the duck pond. They wondered if the goblin might be cooling off in the water, but there was no sign of him.

"You should ask the pigs," a duck quacked helpfully from the reeds. "They've been grumbling all day about something. And pigs are nosy. If there's a goblin on the farm, they'll know about it."

Goldie thanked the duck politely. "I think I can hear the pigs over here," Rachel said, leading the way around the side of the farmhouse.

Soon they could all hear the grunting. The duck was right: the pigs seemed very upset about something.

Goldie perched on the biggest pig's snout. "What's the problem?" she asked kindly.

The pig squinted at the golden fairy in front of his little blue eyes. "It's like this," he began, in a cross, squeaky kind of voice. "It's been so hot that the farmer topped up the mudhole with water, so that us pigs could keep nice and cool."

He twitched his ears indignantly. "But someone else has pinched our spot in the mud – and he won't let us in!"

"It sounds like just the kind of trick a goblin would play!" Rachel declared. "Where's the mudhole?"

The pigs gave directions and the girls set off, with Goldie flying above their heads. Rachel crossed her fingers. She felt quite sure that they would find a goblin in the mud. Who else would be mean enough to stop the pigs from wallowing in their own mud pool?

They hadn't been walking for very long when they heard someone singing in a croaky, tuneless voice:

"I've been having so much fun
Blasting out this golden sun.
It's roasting, toasting, popcorn weather.
Oh, how I love my Sunshine Feather!"

Kirsty, Rachel and Goldie dived behind a nearby tree at once, and carefully peeped out. There, right in the middle of the mudhole, covered in thick, wet mud, was an extremely cheerful goblin. He waved the Sunshine Feather in the air as he sang, and golden sunbeams flooded from its tip, making the air feel even hotter.

"What shall we do?" Kirsty whispered.

Goldie twirled around in frustration. "I hate seeing him with my Sunshine Feather," she muttered. "Look, he's got it all muddy!"

Rachel frowned. "Maybe we could distract him, then dash over and grab the feather while he's looking the other way."

"I don't fancy dashing through that slippery mud," Kirsty said. "We'll probably fall over."

"*Ssshh!*" hissed Goldie suddenly. "What's that noise?"

Kirsty, Rachel and Goldie held their breath as they listened to the strange new sound. It was a loud, wheezing kind of noise, somewhere between a grunt and a hiss.

Grumble-sshhh, it went. *Grumble-sshhh. Grumble-sshhh...*

It was coming from the direction of the mudhole. Kirsty and Rachel peeped out from behind the tree, wondering what sort of terrifying creature they would see.

When Rachel saw what was making the noise, though, she had to clap her hand over her mouth to stop herself laughing out loud.

The wheezy rumble was nothing more than the goblin – snoring!

"At least he isn't singing any more," Kirsty laughed.

Goldie fluttered her wings hopefully when she saw that the goblin was asleep, and she flew a little closer to the Sunshine Feather.

But her face fell when she saw just how tightly the goblin was clutching the feather to his chest. She flew back to the girls, shaking her head. "If I try to pull it out of his grasp, he's sure to wake up," she told them. "How are we going to get that feather?"

A smile appeared on Kirsty's face. Then, without a word, she began running back towards her house. "Back in a minute," she called over her shoulder.

Rachel and Goldie watched her go. They were both dying to know what Kirsty was up to.

Luckily, they didn't have to wait long. When she came back, Kirsty looked quite different!

"What *is* she wearing?" Goldie murmured to Rachel as they saw Kirsty running towards them.

"Her dad's sunglasses," Rachel replied, staring at her friend in surprise. She was starting to wonder if Kirsty had been in the sun for too long. Why had she brought the enormous sunglasses with her? And why was she carrying a fishing rod?

Kirsty grinned at the confused expressions on their faces. "I'll explain everything," she promised, reaching up to rest the fishing rod in the tree. "First, we need to shrink to fairy size, Rachel."

Kirsty and Rachel sprinkled themselves with fairy dust from their lockets. It glittered a bright sunshine-yellow in the light and then – *whoosh*– they were fairy sized! The girls fluttered their wings in delight.

"Now then," Kirsty said. "Let's fly up into the tree and I'll tell you my plan."

They all perched by the fishing rod, and Goldie and Rachel watched as Kirsty's nimble fingers balanced the sunglasses on the end of the fishing hook.

"We're going to let the fishing line out slowly," Kirsty told them quietly, "and lower the sunglasses onto the goblin's nose."

"Why?" Rachel wanted to know.

"Do you think they'll suit him?" Goldie asked.

Kirsty shook her head, trying not to laugh. "With sunglasses on, everything will look dark to him," she explained. "With a bit of luck, he'll think the Sunshine Feather has broken!"

Goldie clapped her hands in delight. "Oh, what a good idea!" she cried. "I love playing tricks on those mean goblins."

Very carefully, Kirsty, Rachel and Goldie turned the wheel of the fishing rod and lowered the sunglasses all the way down to the goblin. Kirsty held her breath as the sunglasses landed right on the end of his nose.

They reeled in the fishing line and then Goldie waved her wand to release a stream of magical fairy dust. Little golden sparkles fizzed and popped like firecrackers around the goblin's head until he woke with a start.

He opened his eyes and blinked when he saw that everything seemed to have gone dark. "My feather's broken!" he moaned, giving it a shake. "Shine, you stupid sun!"

Of course, the Sunshine Feather wasn't broken at all. As soon as the goblin shook it, the sun shone more brilliantly than ever. But as far as the goblin could tell, the world remained in darkness.

He waved the feather again. "I said, shine!" he ordered. The sun shone obediently, as if it were the middle of the day, but the goblin could see no change.

Twice more he shook the feather and twice more the sun shone hotter and brighter, but through the sunglasses, the goblin saw only twilight. As far as he knew, the Sunshine Feather was having no effect.

"Broken!" the goblin finally announced crossly, and he threw the feather away in disgust.

Goldie shot out of the tree at once, like a little golden firework. While the goblin was still muttering gloomily to himself, Goldie swooped down and grabbed the feather.

"Thank you!" she sang happily, hugging it tightly as she flew back to the girls.

With another sprinkle of fairy dust, Rachel and Kirsty turned themselves human again and started scrambling down from the tree with the fishing rod.

The goblin spotted them and jumped to his feet. As he did so, the sunglasses bounced on his nose. "Sunglasses!" he exclaimed, sounding puzzled as he reached up to grab the glasses. He pushed them onto the top of his head and peered at the girls, blinking in the dazzling sunlight.

"You tricked me!" he yelled in fury when he saw Goldie clutching the Sunshine Feather. "Come back with that feather!"

Kirsty and Rachel looked at each other fearfully. The goblin looked very angry at having been outwitted. He shook his fist and ran straight towards the girls.

"*Run!*" shouted Kirsty.

Rachel grabbed Kirsty's hand and they both ran towards the farmhouse as fast as they could. The goblin was right behind them, making a horrible growling sound in his throat.

"Give me back that feather!" he screamed angrily.

Rachel's heart thumped painfully in her chest as she ran. The goblin was closing on them. She could hear his breathing, hoarse and ragged. The goblin stretched out his hand to grab her and she gasped as she felt his fingertips brush her shoulder.

"Got y—" he began. Then his voice turned from anger to confusion. "Hey! What's happening?"

With a swirl of dancing sunbeams, Goldie had waved the Sunshine Feather and pointed it straight at the goblin.

At once, the sun beat down fiercely upon him – and the thick mud that smothered him started drying rapidly. As his legs became stiff and heavy with the solidifying mud, the goblin slowed. Then, as the mud set hard, the goblin found he couldn't move at all.

"No-o-o-!" he wailed in despair.

The girls smiled at the sight of the goblin. "He's a goblin statue!" Rachel exclaimed, laughing.

Kirsty noticed her dad's sunglasses on top of the goblin's head. She took a cautious step towards him. And another. The goblin remained motionless, so she marched right up to him and carefully took the glasses.

"I'll have these back now, I think," she said. "If I'd known how useful these sunglasses were going to be, I'd never have laughed at Dad for wearing them!" she told Rachel.

Goldie and the girls made their way back to the farmhouse where the pigs were waiting expectantly.

"The mudhole is all yours again," Goldie said to the pigs. "You'll find a new goblin scarecrow nearby," she added. "But don't worry. He won't be in any hurry to go back into the mud."

The pigs grunted joyfully and started trotting off in search of their cool mud pool.

Rachel watched them go.

"What will happen to the goblin?" she asked. "He won't have to stay there for ever, will he?"

Goldie's eyes twinkled mischievously. "Not for ever, no," she said. "He'll get out of the mud as soon as it rains."

Now that they were out of danger, Goldie waved the Sunshine Feather with an expert flourish and the sun began to set – just as it was supposed to. The girls watched as the sky was flooded with orange and pink.

"Let's take the Sunshine Feather back to Doodle," Kirsty said happily.

Rachel was yawning. "It's been another busy day, hasn't it?" she smiled.

With the sun setting, the warmth was quickly ebbing away and the girls soon found themselves shivering in their thin T-shirts. Goldie fluttered above them with the Sunshine Feather, tapping it gently to sprinkle sunbeams onto their bare arms and keep them warm.

It was almost dark by the time they got back to Kirsty's garden. They could just about see the silhouette of Doodle perched on the barn roof.

Goldie flew up to give the cockerel back his magic feather. As she did so, Doodle came to life, his fiery feathers glowing brilliant colours in the twilight. He turned to look at Rachel and Kirsty.

"Will come—" he squawked urgently. But, before he could say any more, the magic drained away, his colours faded and he became a rusty old weather-vane once again.

Rachel frowned as she pieced together all the words that Doodle had said so far. "Beware! Jack Frost will come..." she murmured, feeling an icy shiver down her spine as if Jack Frost was already there. "It's a warning, Kirsty!"

Goldie looked worried. "Take care, girls. And thank you," she said. She blew them a stream of fairy kisses that sparkled in the darkening sky. "I must go home now. Goodbye!" She zoomed away into the night and Kirsty and Rachel smiled at each other.

"Only three more feathers to find," Kirsty said. "I wonder which one will be next!"

Evie
the Mist
Fairy

Chapter Five

Evie the Mist Fairy

"Wake up, Rachel!" cried Kirsty, as she jumped out of bed and started to dress.

"I was dreaming that we were back in Fairyland," Rachel said sleepily. "The weather was topsy-turvy and Doodle was trying to sort it out." Doodle, the fairies' magic weather cockerel, had been on Rachel's mind a lot lately!

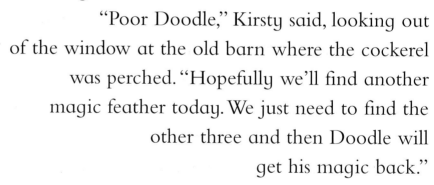

"Poor Doodle," Kirsty said, looking out of the window at the old barn where the cockerel was perched. "Hopefully we'll find another magic feather today. We just need to find the other three and then Doodle will get his magic back."

"Yes," Rachel agreed, brightening at the thought. "But I have to go home in three days, so we don't have long!"

Rachel and Kirsty hurried down to the kitchen. "Did you sleep well?" Kirsty's dad asked.

"Yes, thanks," Rachel replied. As she sat down, she saw a bright green notice on the kitchen table. It read, 'Grand Fun Run at Green Wood Forest, Wetherbury. Everyone welcome.'

She looked at the date. "That's today."

"Yes. Mum's running in it," said Kirsty.

"Why don't you two go and watch?" suggested Mr Tate. "You could give Mum some moral support."

"OK," Rachel and Kirsty agreed happily.

Mr Tate stood up. "I'm going to pick up Gran and take her to the fun run. We might see you there," he told the girls.

"OK, Dad. Goodbye," Kirsty said with a wave.

Just then, Mrs Tate dashed into the kitchen, wearing her jogging kit. She smiled at Kirsty and Rachel. "Sorry, I can't stop, girls. I promised to help mark out the course in the forest."

"That's all right, Mum. We'll follow you up there," Kirsty said.

"We're coming to cheer you on," Rachel explained.

"See you at the woods then!" Mrs Tate called cheerfully as she disappeared out of the door.

A little later, Kirsty and Rachel set out for Green Wood Forest themselves.

"Let's take the river path," Kirsty suggested.

"Oh, yes, we might see some ducklings," Rachel agreed.

As the girls walked up Twisty Lane, sunlight poured through the dancing tree branches and spots of light speckled the road like golden coins. Soon they reached the river. Rachel spotted little puffs of mist rising from the water.

"Look! Do you think that could be fairy mist?" she asked.

"I'm not sure," Kirsty replied. "There's often mist round water, isn't there?"

"Oh, yes, especially in the morning and the evening," Rachel remembered. She felt a little disappointed, but brightened when she saw two swans gliding past, followed by three young cygnets.

Just ahead, Kirsty could see the start of the forest, and something was shimmering on a branch of one of the nearer trees. "What's that?" she asked Rachel.

Rachel went over to look. "I don't know, but it's lovely!" she replied. "Just like angel hair for decorating trees at Christmas."

Kirsty touched a strand of the strange, silvery stuff. It clung to her fingers for a moment, before melting away. "It feels cold!" Kirsty shivered, rubbing her hands together.

Rachel leaned forward for a closer look. Tiny silvery lights shimmered among the fine, silky threads. "I'm sure this is fairy mist," she whispered excitedly.

Kirsty's eyes lit up. "I think you're right," she agreed. She looked up and saw a wispy cloud of the sparkly mist floating gently down towards the trees. "More fairy mist!" Kirsty pointed out. "Come on!"

The girls ran towards a stile that led into the wood. They were out of breath by the time they jumped down onto the forest path and looked around. Wispy, silver mist clung to trees everywhere and coated the grass with tiny droplets. Every twig, leaf and flower glowed and shimmered with a soft silver light. And where the sunbeams reached down through the trees, the fairy mist sparkled with rainbow light.

"Oh!" breathed Rachel. "It's beautiful!"

Kirsty stared open-mouthed at the forest. It looked almost as magical as Fairyland itself!

Slowly, the girls moved forward. After a few steps, Rachel realised that she couldn't see very far ahead. "This mist is building up fast," she said. "The goblin with the Mist Feather must be really nearby."

Kirsty nodded. "You're right," she agreed. "And we can hardly see a thing. The goblin could be right behind us!"

Rachel shivered nervously. Only a couple of minutes had passed, but as the mist grew thicker, the forest began to feel dark and unfriendly. Shadowy figures moved up ahead.

A man wearing a red T-shirt ran out in front of the girls as another runner burst out of the trees. They were heading straight for each other.

"Watch out!" called Kirsty.

But it was too late. *Crash!* The runners bumped into each other. "Sorry. Didn't see you there!" one of them said, rubbing his head.

"I've never seen fog like this in summer," replied the other one.

"What a shame. This fog is ruining the fun run," said Rachel.

Suddenly, something caught Kirsty's eye. "Over there!" she pointed.

A bright light was moving towards them, shining like a lantern. Soon the girls could see that it was a tiny gleaming fairy.

"It's Evie the Mist Fairy!" gasped Kirsty.

"Hello girls," cried Evie as she hovered in the air in front of them. She had long dark hair and she wore a lilac dress with purple boots. Her wand had a sparkly silver tip from which wisps of shimmering mist drifted constantly.

"We're sure that the goblin with the Mist Feather isn't far away," Kirsty told her.

"Yes," agreed Evie, frowning. "And he's causing lots of misty mischief!"

"Could you leave a magic trail behind us, as we go further into the woods?" Rachel asked. "Then we can look for the goblin and still find our way back."

Evie grinned. She waved her wand and a fountain of fairy dust shot out. It floated to the ground and formed a glittering path.

"Now we won't get lost!" she said.

"But we might bump into the runners," Kirsty pointed out. "Let's turn ourselves into fairies, Rachel, then we can fly."

The girls sprinkled themselves with fairy dust from their golden lockets and soon shrank to become fairies with shimmering wings.

Evie rose into the air, a trail of glittering mist streaming from her wand, and the two girls followed her deeper into the forest.

Below them, the runners were still stumbling about in the fog. "Poor Mum. She was really looking forward to today. That nasty goblin's spoiling everyone's fun," said Kirsty crossly. Suddenly, Rachel spotted a dark, hunched shape in the mist below. "Look down there," she called softly. "I think we've found the goblin!"

They all floated down to investigate. The mist was heavy and sticky. It dragged at Rachel's wings as she flew through it. "Oh, it's not a goblin – it's just a dead tree," she sighed, landing on the twisted trunk.

"We may not have found him yet," Kirsty whispered, "but I still think the goblin's nearby. The mist smells nasty and it's like flying through cold porridge!"

Just then, they heard a gruff voice. "It's not fair! I'm cold and I'm lost and I'm hungry!" There was a loud sniff, like a pig snorting. "Poor me!"

Rachel, Kirsty, and Evie looked at each other in excitement.

"That's definitely a goblin speaking!" declared Evie.

"Quick! Let's hide," suggested Rachel.

They hid in the branches of a huge oak and peered down through the leaves. The goblin sat on a log below them. They could see the top of his head and hear a horrible gurgling sound, like slimy stuff going down a plughole.

"Lost in this horrible forest! And I'm so hungry," moaned the goblin, clutching his rumbling tummy. "I'd love some toadstool stew and worm dumplings!"

"Look what he's holding!" whispered Evie.

Kirsty and Rachel saw that a beautiful silvery feather with a lilac tip was clutched in the goblin's stubby fingers. "The Mist Feather!" the girls exclaimed together.

Then Rachel frowned. "If the goblin's lost in the fog, why doesn't he use the magic feather to get rid of it?" she asked.

"Because he doesn't know how," Evie explained. "He's waving the feather about all over the place, which only makes more and more mist."

Just then, one of the runners passed close by. The goblin shot to his feet and hid behind a tree. "It's a…a Pogwurzel!" he whispered in panic. As the sound of the runner's footsteps faded, the goblin peeped out. "Phew! The Pogwurzel's gone," he said and flopped back down on the log, looking about nervously.

"What's a Pogwurzel?" Kirsty asked.

"Pogwurzels are magical, goblin-chasing monsters!" Evie replied.

"Where do they live?" Rachel asked. She and Kirsty had been to Fairyland a few times now, but they had never seen a Pogwurzel.

Evie laughed. "Nowhere!" she said. "Because they don't exist! You see, goblin children can be really naughty, so their mothers tell them that if they don't do as they're told, a Pogwurzel will come and chase them!"

Kirsty and Rachel laughed so much they nearly fell off the branch.

Then Rachel suddenly turned to Kirsty and Evie in excitement. "I've got an idea," she whispered, her eyes shining. "I think I know how we can get the Mist Feather back!"

Evie and Kirsty stared at Rachel. "Tell us!" they pleaded.

Rachel outlined her plan. "If we can convince the goblin that the forest is full of Pogwurzels, he'll do anything to escape. He's bound to want the mist cleared away, so he can find his way out of the wood. Since he's too stupid to  work out how to use the Mist Feather to clear the fog, maybe we can persuade him to give the feather to Evie to let her try."

Evie clapped her hands together in delight. "Then I can keep it and take it back to Doodle!" she said. "It's a brilliant plan!"

"But I'm not sure how we can make the goblin think that there are Pogwurzels in the forest," Rachel added.

The three friends racked their brains.

"I know," Kirsty cried suddenly. "Evie, if you make us human-sized again, Rachel and I can creep up on the goblin from behind, then run past him, screaming that a Pogwurzel is chasing us!"

"Yes, that could work," Evie agreed.

The three friends flew silently down to the ground behind the oak tree. Evie waved her wand and the girls zoomed up to their normal height.

"Ready?" asked Kirsty.

"You bet," Rachel replied firmly.

The girls crept towards the goblin.

"Now!" hissed Rachel.

Kirsty dashed forward. "Help! Help! Save us from the Pogwurzel!" she shouted.

Rachel ran after her. "It's huge and scary and won't leave us alone!" she cried.

The goblin leapt to his feet, his eyes like saucers. "What?" he gasped. "Who are you?"

Kirsty stopped. "Oh, my goodness, a goblin in Pogwurzel Wood!" she exclaimed, pretending to be surprised.

Rachel stopped too. "You must be very brave," she declared.

The goblin's crossed-eyes flicked from Rachel to Kirsty. "Why?" he demanded shakily. "Are their many Pogwurzels around here?"

"Oh, yes," Kirsty chimed in. "Hundreds. This forest is full of them. One of them was chasing us just now," she added, looking nervously over her shoulder. "He'll be along soon I should think."

Just then, Evie fluttered down, her wings shining in the fog. "Pogwurzels especially love to catch goblins, you know. I've heard that they cook them and eat them," she said.

"Eat them!" the goblin's face turned pale with fear.

"Oh, yes. If I was you, I'd get out of this wood right now," Evie went on.

"But I can't," wailed the goblin. "The fog is so thick I can hardly see my own bony toes!" Evie smiled. "I'll help you," she said sweetly. "Just give me that feather you're holding and I'll magic a clear pathway out of the forest for you."

The goblin pinched his nose thoughtfully.

"I don't know. Jack Frost won't like it if I give you the Mist Feather."

"But he's not the one being chased by a Pogwurzel, is he?" Rachel pointed out quickly. "He's not the one who'll be roasted and toasted and turned into Goblin Pie!"

"The Pogwurzels are extra-enormous," Kirsty put in. "And really fierce."

"So is Jack Frost," the goblin said, looking sullen. "I think I'll keep the feather."

Kirsty's heart sank. It looked like the goblin was more stubborn than they had expected. She exchanged looks with Rachel. Now what could they do?

Evie hovered close to the girls. "I've got an idea," she whispered. "You distract the goblin, so he won't notice what I'm doing."

"What are you all talking about?" demanded the goblin suspiciously.

"We think we heard another Pogwurzel," Kirsty replied.

"Where?" the goblin spun round anxiously.

While his back was turned, Evie waved her wand in a complicated pattern. A big fountain of silver and violet sparks shot into a nearby bush, carrying fairy magic there.

"I can hear it! It's coming this way!" Rachel called to the goblin. "Don't believe you," the goblin sneered. "I can't hear it. I bet you never even saw a Pogwurzel in the first place."

"Listen for yourself then," Evie said.

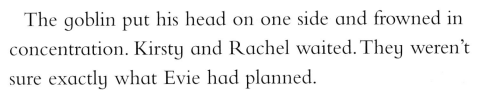

The goblin put his head on one side and frowned in concentration. Kirsty and Rachel waited. They weren't sure exactly what Evie had planned.

Suddenly a deep, scary roar came from the centre of the nearby bush. "Raaghh! I'm a ferocious Pogwurzel! And I really fancy Goblin Pie for supper!"

"Wow! Evie's magical voice is really scary," Kirsty whispered to Rachel.

The goblin stiffened. "Help me, Mummy!" he cried. "A Pogwurzel wants to eat me! I'm sorry I put those toenail clippings in your bed. I won't do it again. Help!" He stumbled behind Kirsty and Rachel, trying to hide. "Don't eat me, Mr Pogwurzel. Eat these girls instead. I bet they taste sweeter than me!"

Evie's magical trick voice came from the bush again. "I only eat goblins," it boomed. "Especially really naughty ones – like you!"

The goblin squealed in alarm and his eyes bulged. He took the Mist Feather from his belt and thrust it at Evie. "Make the mist go away so I can get out of here," he begged. "I don't want to be made into Goblin Pie!"

Evie smiled, took the feather and waved it expertly in the air.

A clear path immediately appeared through the mist. The goblin gave a final terrified glance over his shoulder and then ran away as Kirsty, Rachel and Evie laughed merrily.

"Hurrah! We have the Mist Feather!" Evie declared, waving it over her head.

Silver sparks shot into the air and the mist began to fade. Moments later, the sun shone down onto the forest again.

Rachel and Kirsty beamed. "We can give another magic feather back to Doodle!" Rachel said happily.

"And the fun run should be easier going now," Kirsty put in. "Let's go and see if we can spot Mum before we head home to Doodle."

The three friends made their way towards the fun run course. Runners pounded along between trees marked with big red signs. Everyone could see where they were going now.

"You'd better hide on my shoulder," Rachel said to Evie. Evie nodded and fluttered beneath Rachel's hair.

Suddenly, Kirsty spotted her mum dashing through the trees. Two other runners were close on her heels.

"Come on, Mum!" Kirsty shouted.

"You can do it!" yelled Rachel.

Kirsty's mum threw them a brief smile and waved.

"Not far to go now," she called.

Kirsty and Rachel jumped up and

down with delight. Evie cheered too, but only Rachel could hear her silvery voice.

"Looks like your mum's doing well," said a voice at Kirsty's side.

"Dad! Gran! You're here!" Kirsty exclaimed.

"Only just in time. That fog held us up," said Mr Tate. "Strange how it's completely disappeared now. Almost like magic."

Rachel and Kirsty looked at each other and smiled.

"We're going to head home now," Kirsty told her dad.

"Right you are," he replied. "We'll go and wait for Mum at the finish line."

On the way home, the girls revelled in the glorious sunshine, but Kirsty couldn't help missing the sparkly fairy mist just a little bit.

"Time to give Doodle his feather back," said Rachel, as they reached Kirsty's cottage. "I wonder if he'll speak to us again."

"I hope so," said Kirsty.

Evie flew up to the barn roof. As she slotted the feather into place, the girls watched eagerly.

A fountain of copper and gold sparks fizzed from Doodle's tail. The rusty old weather-vane disappeared and in its place blazed a fiery magic cockerel. Doodle fluffed up his glorious feathers and turned to stare at Rachel and Kirsty.

"If his—" he squawked. But before he could finish the message, his feathers turned to iron and he became an ordinary weather-vane again.

Kirsty frowned. "Beware! Jack Frost will come if his…" she said, putting together all the words Doodle had said so far.

"Jack Frost will come if his *what*?" queried Rachel.

Kirsty shook her head. "We'll just have to find the next feather and hope Doodle can tell us," she sighed.

Evie nodded. "It's important to know the whole message. Jack Frost is dangerous," she warned. "And now I must leave you." She hugged Rachel and Kirsty in turn. "Thank you for helping me."

"You're welcome," chorused both girls.

Evie zoomed up into the brilliant blue sky. Her wand fizzed trails of silver mist, then she was gone.

Kirsty chuckled. "I wonder whose toenail clippings that goblin put in his mum's bed!" she said.

Rachel laughed happily. What an exciting day it had been and there were still two days of her holiday left!

Storm
the Lightning
Fairy

Chapter Six

Storm the Lightning Fairy

"I can't believe tomorrow is my last day here," groaned Rachel. The girls were walking to the park, keen to get outside now the rain had stopped. It had been pouring down all night, but now the sun was shining.

"Put your coats on, though, won't you?" Mrs Tate had told them before they set off. "It looks quite breezy out there."

"It's been such fun, having you to stay," Kirsty told her friend.

"Doodle's got five of his magic feathers back now. But I do hope we find the last two before you go home." Rachel nodded, but before she could say anything, there was a pattering sound and raindrops started splashing down. The girls looked up in dismay to see a huge purple storm cloud covering the sun.

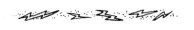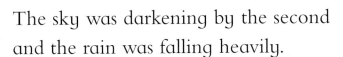
The sky was darkening by the second and the rain was falling heavily.

"Quick!" Kirsty shouted. "Before we get soaked!"

The girls started to run, and Rachel put her hands over her head as raindrops pelted them from all sides. "Where are we going?" she yelled.

"Let's just find some shelter," Kirsty replied, grabbing Rachel's hand and pulling her along. "I'm soaked already!"

The girls stopped under a large chestnut tree near the park entrance. The tree's wide, leafy branches gave good cover. "Great idea," shivered Rachel, trying to shake the raindrops from her coat.

But just as she said that, there was a deafening rumble of thunder, followed by an almighty *FLASH!* The whole sky was lit up by a

blast of lightning. Kirsty and Rachel watched in alarm as a lightning bolt slammed straight into the tree. "We need to get away from here quickly," Kirsty cried, jumping back in fright. "It's dangerous to be under trees in a thunder storm!"

"Wait a minute," Rachel said, staring at the branch.

Rain was pouring off her shoulders but she didn't seem to notice. "Kirsty, look. The branch is... *sparkling*."

And so it was. The leaves were shining a bright, glittering green, glowing against the darkness of the day. Tiny twinkling lights were flickering all over the bark of the branch. It reminded Kirsty of the trees they'd seen in Fairyland. And that made her think that maybe...

"It's a *magical* storm!" Kirsty exclaimed in delight, her eyes almost as bright as the shining leaves. "Look at the sky, Rachel!"

Both girls gazed up in wonder as the lightning flashed again, and a million sparkling lights danced around the thunder clouds before fading away into the darkness.

Rachel grinned with excitement. "It's magical, but very wet!" she laughed. "Let's find somewhere drier and safer. Come on!"

The two girls charged away from the park along the road. Rather than run all the way home, Kirsty pointed ahead. "Let's shelter in there!" she cried.

Rachel blinked the raindrops from her eyelashes as she followed her friend up the path of a large building. 'Wetherbury Museum', she read on a small blue sign. Kirsty pulled the double doors open and she and Rachel tumbled inside. "Phew!" Rachel whistled. "Talk about stormy weather!"

Kirsty was looking thoughtful. "It must be the goblin with the Lightning Feather who's behind this," she said. "He has to be close by, don't you think?"

"Definitely," Rachel agreed. "I—" Before she could say anything else, she was interrupted by a deafening *ROOOAAARRR!* Rachel clutched Kirsty's arm. "What was that?" she whispered.

Kirsty smiled. "I should have warned you – there's a dinosaur display in here," she said. "Some dinosaur bones were found in Wetherbury, and the museum has an enormous model of how the dinosaur would have looked. It roars and moves. Come on, I'll show you."

Kirsty led Rachel into one of the museum galleries. A group of people were being shown around by a tour guide. Kirsty pointed to an enormous model dinosaur.

Rachel stared at the long neck, broad body and huge tail of the model. The dinosaur was standing in water that was clearly supposed to represent a river. Spiky rubber fish floated around its feet. "Wow!" she exclaimed.

Kirsty grinned. "Watch this," she said, and pressed a big red button. The dinosaur leaned down and opened its jaws. It snapped up one of the fish, then lifted up its head so that the fish tumbled down into its belly.

"That's brilliant!" Rachel said, laughing. "What happens if you press this blue button?"

RROOOOOAAARRRR!

"That's what happens," Kirsty giggled. As the dinosaur's roar faded, Rachel overheard the tour guide. "Listen!" she hissed to Kirsty.

"…don't know where this fairy exhibit has come from," the guide was saying in a puzzled voice. She shrugged. "I've just come back from holiday – it must be a new display. Maybe somebody's discovered that fairies were around at the same time as dinosaurs!" The group laughed politely. "Anyway, let's move on."

Rachel and Kirsty crept to the back of the tour group to look at the fairy exhibit. There seemed to be a tiny shape in a glass case, but they couldn't quite make out what it was.

As the group followed the tour guide out of the room, there was another growl of thunder and the girls saw a flash of lightning at the windows. Once again the sky seemed to glitter with a stream of dancing silver sparkles. Then, all the lights went out inside the museum.

"Oh dear, it's a power cut," the guide said as her tour group gasped. "Follow me, everyone – I think we have some torches in a cupboard through here."

Rachel and Kirsty waited until the group had left the room, then went to take a closer look at the display case. There inside was a real fairy – and she was waving frantically at them!

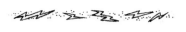

"It's Storm the Lightning Fairy!" cried Rachel, opening the case. "Hello," said Storm in relief. "I'm really glad to see you two!" Storm had long white-gold hair and she wore a striking purple trouser suit. A golden lightning strike hung on a chain around her neck, and her purple wand sent out little crackling lightning bolts whenever it moved.

"Hello, Storm," said Kirsty. "What were you doing in there?"

Storm tossed her hair. "The goblin with the Lightning Feather shut me in," she explained crossly. "He's somewhere in the museum. Have you seen all the lightning he's made?" She put her hands on her hips. "Please help me get the feather back. Lightning is powerful stuff, you know."

"We know," Rachel told her.

"Someone's coming," Storm whispered suddenly. "It might be the goblin. Hide!"

The girls pressed themselves back against the wall and Storm swooped down onto Kirsty's shoulder.

The door creaked open and the goblin came in. Kirsty thought he was a particularly scary-looking one – with extra-narrow eyes, long pointed ears and a thin, bony body. The lights were still out in the museum, but the goblin soon lit up the room. He was waving the Lightning Feather around so gleefully that golden

bolts of lightning whizzed all over the place, crackling and fizzing, and sending electric blue sparks shooting from everything they touched.

Storm put her head in her hands. "I can hardly bear to watch," she groaned. "What does that stupid goblin think he's doing?"

"Oh!" gasped Rachel, ducking down as a lightning bolt zoomed past her head. "We've got to stop him before he does any damage," she hissed.

"Who said that?" the goblin snapped. "Fairy, was that you? Or is somebody else in here?"

Kirsty's heart pounded so loudly she was sure the goblin was going to hear it. He was turning around, looking everywhere to see who'd made the noise.

At last, his eyes fell upon the girls and he grinned a horrible grin. "Oho!" he cried. "Planning to sneak up on me, were you?" And with a wave of the feather, he sent three fiery lightning bolts whizzing towards them!

The girls threw themselves behind a display case and the lightning crashed to the ground, missing them by a few centimetres. Wisps of glittering smoke rose in coils from a scorch mark on the floor, and drifted up to the ceiling where they fizzled out in a shower of blue sparks. Fairy lightning was certainly powerful stuff!

Rachel bit her lip. They needed a plan – and fast! "I'll just peep out to see where the goblin is," she whispered.

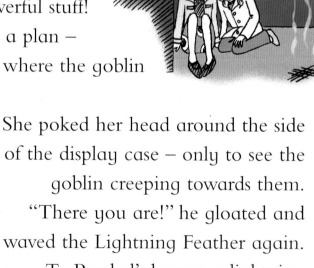

She poked her head around the side of the display case – only to see the goblin creeping towards them. "There you are!" he gloated and waved the Lightning Feather again. To Rachel's horror, a lightning bolt came shooting straight towards her face!

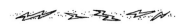 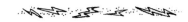

Rachel leapt back behind the display case just in time. The lightning bolt whizzed so close to her, it singed the hem of her coat.

Storm fluttered up, a determined look on her face. "Shrink to fairy size, girls!" she called. "It'll be harder for him to blast you when you're small."

Kirsty opened her locket, and sprinkled fairy dust all over herself. Seconds later, she was the same size as Storm. She shook out her wings at once and pirouetted in the air.

"I can't find my locket," Rachel said anxiously.

Kirsty gasped as she saw it shining on the floor under a display case, out of Rachel's reach. She pointed it out to her friend. "It must have fallen off when you dived for cover!" she cried.

Before Kirsty could fly down and grab the locket, the goblin came lumbering over. He was so close now that he was almost next to Rachel. He held the feather tightly in his hand and Rachel could see a wicked glint in his eye.

"Help!" she cried, dodging neatly to one side and running away. "Can you distract him, Storm?"

Storm was whizzing through the air, trying to get close enough to Rachel to magic her into a fairy – but the goblin was blocking her way.

And he was still waving the feather around, sending lightning bolts flashing in every direction. It was too dangerous for Kirsty or Storm to get any closer to their friend.

"What are we going to do?" Kirsty wailed as she watched Rachel running away from the goblin. She racked her brains for a way to save her friend, and suddenly spotted a large mirror hanging on one wall. An idea came to her. A crazy idea! But she thought it might just work...

Kirsty pointed up at the mirror. "Would lightning be strong enough to break that?" she asked Storm quickly.

Storm shook her head. "No, fairy lightning isn't like normal lightning. It would just bounce back off a mirror," she replied.

Kirsty grinned. "Perfect," she said. "I'm going to try to surprise the goblin. You get ready to grab the feather!"

Kirsty could tell from Rachel's face that her friend was starting to get tired, so she flew down towards the goblin at once. He was just stretching out a bony hand to grab Rachel's coat, when Kirsty tugged hard on one of his ears.

"Ow! Who did that?" he yelped, jumping back angrily.

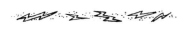

Kirsty fluttered up in front of the mirror. "Coo-ee! Over here!" she yelled, waving cheekily. "Catch me if you can!"

She saw the goblin aim the Lightning Feather straight at her. "Cheeky little fairy," he yelled. "Take that!" And at once, another crackling lightning bolt shot towards Kirsty.

Kirsty held her breath as she watched it whizz through the air. It was so close she could practically feel its scorching heat on her face...

"Move!" Rachel shouted in panic, terrified that her brave friend was going to get hit.

But Kirsty waited until the very last second, and then, just as the lightning was about to strike her, she dodged out of its way.

The fairy lightning struck the mirror and, as Storm had predicted, it bounced right back – straight at the goblin!

"Help!" he shouted, trying to get out of its way. He tripped clumsily over his own feet and fell to the ground beneath the dinosaur model – dropping the Lightning Feather as he did so!

Quick as a flash, Storm picked up the precious feather and flew high in the air, well out of the reach of goblin fingers! "Nice work, Kirsty!" she cheered triumphantly.

"Hey!" yelled the goblin in fury, jumping up to try and reach the feather. He fell awkwardly against the dinosaur, lost his balance and tumbled right into the water tray, with the rubber fish! Grinning mischievously, Storm pointed the Lightning Feather at the dinosaur. A stream of lightning bolts struck the red and blue buttons on the control panel. Rachel's eyes widened in delight as the dinosaur sparkled all over for a second, and then...

"RROOOOAAARRRRRR!" went the dinosaur, opening its jaws. And with that, it bent down and snatched up the goblin in its teeth!

Rachel, Kirsty and Storm watched in amazement as the dinosaur lifted its head with the struggling goblin still in its mouth.

"Put me down!" the goblin raged. "Aaaaargghh!"

Of course, the model took no notice of the goblin but obediently went through its usual process.

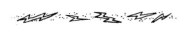 

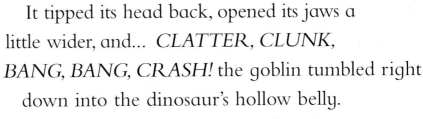

It tipped its head back, opened its jaws a little wider, and... *CLATTER, CLUNK, BANG, BANG, CRASH!* the goblin tumbled right down into the dinosaur's hollow belly.

A furious hammering immediately started up inside the model. "Let me out!" yelled the goblin.

Laughing with delight, Kirsty sprinkled another pinch of fairy dust over herself. Soon she felt her wings disappear and her legs grow and she was back to being a girl once more.

She went straight over to Rachel. "Are you all right?" she asked. "That was scary!"

"Yes," Rachel agreed. "But we managed it, thanks to your brilliant idea, Kirsty. Now we've got Doodle's sixth feather!"

Storm flew over with Rachel's magical locket. "Here you are," she said, handing it over. "And I think we'd better leave while we can," she added nervously. "It sounds like

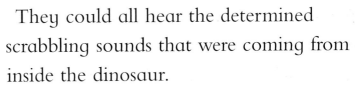

the goblin's trying to climb out."

They could all hear the determined scrabbling sounds that were coming from inside the dinosaur.

Rachel fastened her locket carefully around her neck as the friends headed for the exit.

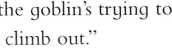

"I can't believe I missed out on being a fairy today," she said with a sigh. "That's the only bad part. That – and nearly getting blasted by fairy lightning!" she finished with a smile.

The girls and Storm rushed out of the museum. Outside, the bad weather had passed, the rain had stopped and the dark clouds seemed to be melting away. The sun came out and made the wet pavement glisten.

Rachel glanced down and groaned. "Oh, no," she said. "My coat! I'd forgotten it had been singed by the goblin's lightning."

Kirsty saw that the coat was blackened and scorched, and the stitching had frazzled away.

"Mum's going to go mad," Rachel said.

"Let me see," said Storm, darting down for a closer look. As soon as she saw the problem, she smiled and gently stroked her magic wand over the material. A trail of twinkling lights glimmered over the scorch mark, and then the coat was as good as new!

"Thank you, Storm," Rachel gasped in delight.

Storm winked. "I should be the one thanking you two," she said. "Doodle will be so pleased to have another feather back in his tail!"

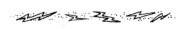 

They hurried down Twisty Lane to Kirsty's house.

"There's Doodle," Kirsty told Storm, pointing to the weather-vane on the old barn.

Storm flew up to return the Lightning Feather to Doodle's tail, and the girls waited expectantly. What was Doodle going to say this time?

As Storm carefully slotted the Lightning Feather into place, Doodle's iron feathers softened and shimmered with a thousand fiery colours. His head turned towards the girls and his beak opened. "…goblins fail!" he squawked urgently.

Then, as fast as he had come to life, the colour vanished from his feathers and he was an ordinary weather-vane once more.

Rachel and Kirsty looked at one another in alarm.

"Beware! Jack Frost will come if his goblins fail!" they cried together.

Storm looked worried, too. "If you find the Rain Feather, then Jack Frost's goblins will have failed," she said. "That doesn't sound good." She fluttered down to Kirsty and Rachel. "You must be careful, girls. Jack Frost is very sneaky."

"We know," Kirsty said, biting her lip. "And we will be careful."

Kirsty and Rachel hugged Storm goodbye. Then they watched as the Lightning Fairy flew away into the distance. The girls stood in silence for a moment, both thinking about Doodle's warning.

"We've outwitted Jack Frost before," Kirsty said bravely. "I'm sure we can do it again."

Rachel grinned. "You bet," she agreed. "Watch out, Jack Frost! We're ready for you!" she shouted.

Hayley

the Rain Fairy

Chapter Seven

Hayley the Rain Fairy

"I'm awake," said Kirsty sleepily, reaching out to turn off her alarm clock. *That's strange,* she thought, *the alarm isn't ringing.*

"Quack, quack, quack!" The noise that had woken her up came again. Now that Kirsty was awake, she realised that the sound was coming from outside. She jumped out of bed and peeped between the curtains.

"Oh!" she cried. There was water right up to her windowsill, and a large brown duck was swimming past, followed by five fluffy ducklings!

Kirsty rushed over to her best friend. "Wake up, Rachel!" she said.

Rachel sat up sleepily. "What's going on?" she asked.

"I think the river must have overflowed. Wetherbury is flooded!" replied Kirsty.

"Really?" Rachel was wide awake now. She looked out of the window. "That's odd," she said, pointing. "The water isn't so deep in the garden and the lane. How can it be right up to your bedroom window at the same time?"

"Maybe it's fairy weather magic!" Kirsty gasped, her eyes shining.

"Of course!" Rachel agreed. She knew that fairy magic followed its own rules.

"It's the last day of your stay, so we have to find the magic Rain Feather today," Kirsty called over her shoulder, as she got dressed. "At least with all this magical flooding, we can be sure the goblin who stole it isn't far away!"

As Rachel hurriedly threw on some clothes, there was a tapping noise at the window. "What if that's the goblin?" she whispered, nervously.

Kirsty peeped cautiously out of the window, then threw back the curtains with a smile. An elegant white swan was tapping on the window with its beak. And a tiny fairy was sitting on the swan's back, waving at the girls.

"It's Hayley the Rain Fairy!" Rachel gasped in delight.

Kirsty was just about to open the window
and let Hayley in when she hesitated. "All
the water will rush inside," she said.

Hayley laughed. "Don't worry," she
called. "It's fairy rain. It won't spill into
people's houses."

So, slowly, Kirsty opened the window. The water stayed where
it was.

Hayley fluttered into the air and blew the swan a kiss. "Thanks for
the ride!" she said. "Goodbye!" The swan
dipped its head and glided away.

"Hello, girls," Hayley sang happily. She
wore a pretty violet sarong-style skirt, and
a matching top. Her long dark hair was
tied up in a ponytail and decorated with
a bright blue flower. She folded her arms
and little droplets of blue and violet
scattered from her silver wand. "Now, it's
time that nasty goblin gave Doodle's
Rain Feather back!" she said firmly.

"We think so too," Rachel agreed. "But how can we go looking
for him with all this flooding? We need a boat."

"I helped Dad clear out the loft last week and we found an old
dinghy," Kirsty said eagerly. "Let's go and ask if we can take it out
to play."

Hayley flew onto Rachel's shoulder and hid beneath her hair, as the girls went downstairs.

Mrs Tate was in the kitchen. "Hello, girls," she said. "Your dad's trying to work out why the water isn't flooding into the house. But I'm just glad the place is dry! Toast's made. Help yourselves."

"Thanks, Mum." Kirsty picked up some toast. "Is it OK if we go out in the old dinghy?"

Mrs Tate smiled. "Sounds fine to me."

Kirsty and Rachel rushed out to the garage, munching toast as they went. It didn't take long to inflate the dinghy, and then the girls put it out of the window onto the water. They climbed in carefully. It was just big enough for two people.

"Perfect!" said Hayley, sitting on the front of the dinghy like a tiny sparkling figurehead.

The girls paddled the dinghy towards the High Street. Outside the Post Office, they saw a group of children splashing about happily. But not everyone was so pleased about the water.

Kirsty spotted a cat that had sought refuge in an oak tree on the village green. "Poor thing," she said. "At least it's safe up there."

The girls paddled on towards the park. Rachel saw a strange shape floating out from behind the children's slide. "Look over there. It's an upturned umbrella!" she said, pointing.

Kirsty's eyes widened. Four ducks, in a brightly-coloured harness, were quacking crossly and pulling an umbrella boat along. Inside sat a bedraggled figure.

Suddenly Rachel realised who it was. "It's the goblin," she gasped. "And he'll see us at any moment!"

"Quick, hide!" Hayley shouted.

Kirsty and Rachel looked round desperately. The hut next to the bowling green was too far away and the goblin was approaching rapidly. There was nowhere to hide.

"If we become fairies, we can hide in the trees!" Kirsty suggested quickly.

Rachel was already taking out her locket. Kirsty found hers too and the girls sprinkled themselves with fairy dust. They soon felt themselves shrinking and delicate fairy wings appeared on their backs. Then they zoomed upwards and landed in the tree.

Rachel spotted an empty bird's nest. "Quick! In here!" she whispered.

Kirsty and Hayley jumped in beside Rachel. The nest was lined with moss and feathers. It felt really cosy and dry.

They weren't a moment too soon. The goblin in his umbrella boat floated beneath the tree. One of the ducks flapped its wings angrily, pulling at the stripy harness. The umbrella wobbled and almost tipped up.

"Oo-er! I nearly fell out then!" the goblin complained. "Stop trying to get away, you stupid ducks. You've got my lovely warm scarf for a harness. It's me that's freezing! Atchoo!"

Kirsty, Rachel and Hayley kept as quiet as they could while they peeped out of the nest. The goblin shivered and sniffed and moaned to himself.

"It's not fair. I wanted the Sunshine Feather, and instead I get stuck with this horrible Rain Feather! I should be toasty warm, not cold as yesterday's mud porridge! Atchoo!"

"He's got a really nasty cold," murmured Hayley.

"Serves him right!" Kirsty replied.

Just then, the goblin lifted his hat and drew out a beautiful copper feather with silvery streaks. He jabbed it crossly into the air. "Stop this rain, right now!" he uttered irritably. The rain stopped at once and the goblin grinned.

"At least it does as it's told," he grunted, stuffing the feather back under his hat.

"Oh, the poor Rain Feather!" whispered Hayley, indignantly.

Suddenly the goblin's miserable face lit up in a grin. He had spotted the girls' dinghy.

"Oh, goody, a real boat just for me!" he cried. Using his big hands as paddles, the goblin steered alongside the dinghy. Then he bunched up

his long legs, sprang straight up in the air and landed, plonk, in the dinghy.

"Nice duckies. Let's harness you to my new boat," he wheedled.

"That's it. All ready now. Off we go!"

"Cheeky thing! He's stealing our dinghy!" Kirsty exclaimed. "And using the umbrella over his head."

"I feel like some more rain now!" shouted the goblin happily. He took out the Rain Feather and waved it in the air. A big grey cloud appeared and rain began to pour down. "Faster, ducks, faster!" urged the goblin, his voice growing fainter as the dinghy sailed out of sight.

Rachel, Kirsty, and Hayley watched in dismay. "How are we going to get the Rain Feather back now?" Rachel wailed.

Kirsty stood up. "I've got a plan!" she announced.

"Hurrah! What is it?" Hayley asked.

"Remember how the goblin said he wanted the Sunshine Feather?" Kirsty explained. "Well, if we can find a feather that looks like the Sunshine Feather, then we might be able to trick the goblin into swapping!"

"It's a good plan. But where can we get a feather from?" Rachel said thoughtfully. "The magic feathers are really long and beautiful."

Kirsty grinned and flew into the air. "Follow me!"

Hayley and Rachel zoomed after Kirsty as she led them back over her house and towards the farmyard.

The farmhouse and cowshed were centimetres deep in water. Kirsty flew down and swooped through the henhouse door with Hayley and Rachel close behind. Inside, they saw fluffy shapes huddled on a perch above the waterlogged floor.

"Excuse me," Hayley said politely to the chickens. "We need your help."

The chickens looked up with dull eyes. "Eggs all wet. Feet cold and muddy. Feathers all soggy…" they squawked, sullenly.

"Oh, dear. They seem so sad," Hayley sighed.

"It's the wet. Dad says chickens really hate it," Kirsty explained.

Hayley flew down to stroke the chickens' heads. "Don't worry, chickens. We can make this rain stop with your help," she told them brightly.

"We need a big feather, as long as this…" Kirsty said, spreading out her hands to show what she meant.

"Why didn't you say so?" squawked

a handsome cockerel. He twisted round and plucked a feather from his tail. "Will this do?"

"Oh, yes. It's gorgeous. Thank you," Hayley said, fluttering down to take the feather. "Now, cheer up," she said, flying towards the door with Rachel and Kirsty. "We're going to go and stop the rain!"

The chickens fluffed themselves up, already looking much happier. They lifted their wings to wave after the girls.

"Goodbye!" they clucked. Outside, on the henhouse roof, Hayley, Rachel and Kirsty looked at the long coppery feather. "I don't think the goblin will be fooled," Hayley said doubtfully. "The Sunshine Feather is flecked with golden yellow."

Kirsty grinned. "No problem. There's a tin of yellow paint in our garage."

They all rushed back to the garage, and Kirsty painted yellow speckles on the feather.

"Perfect! It looks just like the Sunshine Feather!" exclaimed Hayley in delight.

"Now all we have to do is find the goblin," said Rachel.

Just then, a group of ducks flew overhead. Without a word, Hayley rose up in a cloud of violet sparkles. Rachel and Kirsty watched as she flew alongside the ducks.

Soon she was back. "The ducks have seen the goblin in the field behind the museum!" Hayley declared. "Come on!"

The girls followed Hayley to the back of the museum and, sure enough, there was the goblin floating across the flooded field in Kirsty's dinghy.

"Atchoo!" he spluttered loudly.

Hayley, Kirsty and Rachel hovered near the goblin.

"I've got something you might like," Hayley called to the goblin, waving the fake Sunshine Feather.

The goblin's eyes lit up greedily. "The Sunshine Feather! Give it here!" His long arm shot out and his fingers grabbed for the feather, but Hayley sped backwards out of his reach. "I'll swap my feather for yours, if you like," she offered sweetly. Rachel and Kirsty held their breath. Would the goblin fall for their trick?

"OK," said the goblin.

Hayley zoomed down and took the Rain Feather, thrusting the pretend Sunshine Feather at the goblin. He grabbed it and stroked it fondly.

Hayley immediately waved the Rain Feather in a complicated pattern. "Rain, stop!" she ordered. The rain stopped and the sun came out, turning the shallow pools and puddles into molten gold.

The goblin waved his feather triumphantly. "My Sunshine Feather's working already!" he boasted. "I'm off now. It's about time I had a holiday." He leapt out of the dinghy and splashed away across the field.

Rachel, Kirsty, and Hayley hugged each other happily.

"We did it!" Kirsty exclaimed.

"Yes, now we can return this last feather to Doodle and he can take charge of Fairyland's weather again," said Rachel. Kirsty was about to turn towards home, when she suddenly shivered.

"That's strange. It's getting really cold," she said. Rachel looked alarmed.

"Oh, no! Remember Doodle's warning? He said 'Beware! Jack Frost will come if his goblins fail!'"

There was a crackling noise as the floodwater stopped draining away and started to freeze. Hayley paled. "It's Jack Frost," she squealed. "He's coming!"

A tall, bony figure suddenly appeared out of thin air. Icicles hung from his eyebrows and beard. "You again!" he snarled at Kirsty and Rachel. "How dare you meddle in my affairs?"

Rachel, Kirsty and Hayley gasped in fear as Jack Frost towered over them.

Kirsty looked at Hayley. "Go!" she whispered. "Take the Rain Feather to Doodle."

Hayley looked reluctant to leave, but she nodded and zoomed away.

"As for you – you useless goblin!" Jack Frost was saying. "I'll give you a holiday you won't forget!" He lifted his wand and sent a blast of freezing white light towards the goblin, who was stomping across the field. There was a fizz and a crackle and the goblin became a skinny, ice statue!

Jack Frost turned back to face the girls and gave a shriek of rage when he saw that Hayley had gone. He glowered at Kirsty who

was reaching for her locket. "No you don't!" he snapped. He pointed his wand and a narrow beam of light shot out, freezing both lockets tightly shut.

"Oh!" cried Rachel and Kirsty. Without their fairy dust, they would have to stay fairy-sized!

Jack Frost looked down at the two tiny girls. "What's the matter? Cold frozen your tongues?" he asked, laughing nastily. It sounded like footsteps crunching snail shells. "Well, you two have interfered once too often. It's time I got rid of you for good!" he said, raising his wand.

Rachel grabbed Kirsty's arm and pulled her behind a tree, just as an icy blast shot towards them. There was a loud snapping sound and thick white ice coated the trunk.

Jack Frost stepped round the tree and raised his wand again. Rachel heard a rushing sound and squeezed her eyes shut, expecting to feel an icy blast at any moment…

But, instead, Rachel heard Jack Frost give a scream of rage, so she opened her eyes. Doodle, the fairy cockerel, was approaching in a great rush of wind and fire. His magnificent tail glittered with sparks of red and gold and copper. "Get away from them, Jack Frost!" he ordered, his beak snapping with rage. He flapped his wings and a stream of white-hot sparks sprayed from them and sizzled on the ice. "Ouch! Stop that!" cried Jack Frost, backing away as several sparks landed on his robe.

"Doodle's come to save us!" breathed Kirsty, as Hayley flew down to join the girls. "And he's his true fairy-self again!"

Doodle swept Rachel, Kirsty, and Hayley under one wing. Then he peered down his beak at Jack Frost. "You must pay for what you've done!" he said severely. "You have brought havoc to the weather, and you have threatened two of Fairyland's dearest friends!"

Jack Frost cowered. Melting ice ran down his face and dripped from his chin. "They shouldn't have stuck their noses into my business," he sulked.

"What if Jack Frost casts a spell on Doodle?" Rachel asked anxiously.

Hayley shook her head. "Now he has all his feathers back, Doodle is seven times as powerful as any one fairy. He's more than a match for Jack Frost!"

Doodle fluttered his magic tail feathers. Coloured sparks shot out and a rainbow began rising from the ground.

Jack Frost started spinning helplessly round and round. "Stop! Help!" he cried, as the rainbow swept him up into the sky in a brilliant arc. Jack Frost struggled and yelled, but he was soon a distant speck amidst the glowing colours.

Kirsty and Rachel were still staring after him when they felt themselves being whisked up in a whirlwind of shimmering fairy dust. With Hayley and Doodle, they sped through a blue sky dotted with clouds.

"It's Fairyland!" breathed Rachel with delight, as she saw the turrets of the fairy palace gleaming in the sunshine!

A crowd of fairies waved and cheered as Doodle and the girls landed in the courtyard of the palace. King Oberon and Queen Titania were waiting to greet them.

"Welcome back, Doodle," said the King and Queen warmly. "And our heartfelt thanks to you, Rachel and Kirsty."

"What's going to happen to Jack Frost, Your Majesties?" Kirsty asked.

Titania looked stern. "He can stay at the end of the rainbow until he sees the error of his ways. He's gone too far this time," she said.

Kirsty and Rachel smiled with relief. That should keep him out of mischief for a while, Rachel thought. "We'd better give our magic lockets back," she said to Kirsty.

Oberon shook his head. "You must keep them." He

waved his hand over the lockets. Silver sprinkles shot out of his fingers and tiny bells rang. "I have filled them with new fairy dust. If you ever need help yourselves, this dust will whisk you straight to Fairyland."

"Where you will always be welcome," added Titania, with a sweet smile.

Kirsty and Rachel's eyes opened wide. This was a great honour!

Then Doodle came forward. "I have a gift for you, too," he said, and gave them a weather-vane that looked just like him.

"Thank you," said the girls. They hugged each of the Weather Fairies and said goodbye to Doodle and the Fairy King and Queen. Then a whirlwind of sparkling fairy dust swept them upwards, and in a few moments they landed back in Kirsty's garden.

Mr Tate appeared from behind the barn, looking puzzled. "Oh, good, you've found that old weather-vane. Where was it?"

"It appeared by magic," Kirsty told him, and Rachel smiled.

Mr Tate laughed. "Well, I'd better put it back. I've got used to seeing it up there."

"Me too," Kirsty agreed.

Just as Mr Tate was putting the weather-vane up, a car turned into the drive.

"It's Mum and Dad!" Rachel said, waving.

"Hello, you two. Have you had a good week?" asked Mr and Mrs Walker, as they climbed out of the car.

"The best! It's been really magical!" Rachel replied.

The girls went upstairs to get Rachel's things, while their parents had tea in the kitchen. Then it was time for Rachel to leave. Kirsty hugged her friend goodbye.

"You must come and visit soon," Mrs Walker told Kirsty.

"Yes, do!" Rachel added.

"I'd love to, thanks," Kirsty smiled. "Goodbye, Rachel!"

After Rachel had gone, Kirsty stood in the garden thinking about all their adventures. She looked up at the barn roof. For a moment, a shining rainbow touched the old tiles and the weather-vane spun round swiftly. As it did so, Kirsty thought she saw the cockerel wink at her cheekily, and sparkle with fairy magic.

The Rainbow Fairies

Ruby the Red Fairy – 978-1-84362-016-7
Amber the Orange Fairy – 978-1-84362-017-4
Saffron the Yellow Fairy – 978-1-84362-018-1
Fern the Green Fairy – 978-1-84362-019-8
Sky the Blue Fairy – 978-1-84362-020-4
Izzy the Indigo fairy – 978-1-84362-021-1
Heather the Violet Fairy – 978-1-84362-022-8

The Weather Fairies

Crystal the Snow Fairy – 978-1-84362-633-6
Abigail the Breeze Fairy – 978-1-84362-634-3
Pearl the Cloud Fairy – 978-1-84362-635-0
Goldie the Sunshine Fairy – 978-1-84362-641-1
Evie the Mist Fairy – 978-1-84362-636-7
Storm the Lightning Fairy – 978-1-84362-637-4
Hayley the Rain Fairy – 978-1-84362-638-1

The Party Fairies

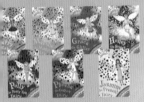

Cherry the Cake Fairy – 978-1-84362-818-7
Melodie the Music Fairy – 978-1-84362-819-4
Grace the Glitter Fairy – 978-1-84362-820-0
Honey the Sweet Fairy – 978-1-84362-821-7
Polly the Party Fun Fairy – 978-184362-822-4
Phoebe the Fashion Fairy – 978-184362-823-1
Jasmine the Present Fairy – 978-1-84362-824-8

The Jewel Fairies

India the Moonstone Fairy – 978-1-84362-958-0
Scarlett the Garnet Fairy – 978-1-84362-954-2
Emily the Emerald Fairy – 978-1-84362-955-9
Chloe the Topaz Fairy – 978-1-84362-956-6
Amy the Amethyst Fairy – 978-1-84362-957-3
Sophie the Sapphire Fairy – 978-184362-953-5
Lucy the Diamond Fairy – 978-1-84362-959-7

The Pet Keeper Fairies

Katie the Kitten Fairy – 978-1-84616-166-7
Bella the Bunny Fairy – 978-1-84616-170-4
Georgia the Guinea Pig Fairy – 978-1-84616-168-1
Lauren the Puppy Fairy – 978-1-84616-169-8
Harriet the Hamster Fairy – 978-1-84616-167-4
Molly the Goldfish Fairy – 978-1-84616-172-8
Penny the Pony Fairy – 978-1-84616-171-1

The Fun Day Fairies

Megan the Monday Fairy – 978-1-84616-188-9
Tallulah the Tuesday Fairy – 978-1-84616-189-6
Willow the Wednesday Fairy – 978-1-84616-190-2
Thea the Thursday Fairy – 978-1-84616-191-9
Freya the Friday Fairy – 978-1-84616-192-6
Sienna the Saturday Fairy – 978-1-84616-193-3
Sarah the Sunday Fairy – 978-1-84616-194-0

The Petal Fairies

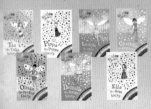

Tia the Tulip Fairy – 978-1-84616-457-6
Pippa the Poppy Fairy – 978-1-84616-458-3
Louise the Lily Fairy – 978-1-84616-459-0
Charlotte the Sunflower Fairy – 978-184616-460-6
Danielle the Daisy Fairy – 978-1-84616-462-0
Olivia the Orchid Fairy – 978-1-84616-461-3
Ella the Rose Fairy – 978-1-84616-464-4

The Dance Fairies

Bethany the Ballet Fairy – 978-1-84616-490-3
Jade the Disco Fairy – 978-1-84616-491-0
Rebecca the Rock 'N' Roll Fairy – 978-1-8461
Tasha the Tap Dance Fairy – 978-1-84616-49
Jessica the Jazz Fairy – 978-1-84616-495-8
Saskia the Salsa Fairy – 978-1-84616-496-5
Imogen the Ice Dance Fairy – 978-1-84616-4

The Sporty Fairies

Helena the Horseriding Fairy – 978-1-84616-
Francesca the Football Fairy – 978-1-84616-8
Zoe the Skating Fairy – 978-1-84616-890-1
Naomi the Netball Fairy – 978-1-84616-891
Samantha the Swimming Fairy – 978-184616
Alice the Tennis Fairy – 978-184616-893-2
Gemma the Gymnastics Fairy – 978-184616-

The Music Fairies

Poppy the Piano Fairy – 978-140830-033-6
Ellie the Guitar Fairy – 978-140830-030-5
Fiona the Flute Fairy – 978-140830-029-9
Danni the Drum Fairy – 978-140830-028-2
Maya the Harp Fairy – 978-1-40830-031-2
Victoria the Violin Fairy – 978-1-40830-027-
Sadie the Saxophone Fairy – 978-1-40830-0

The Magical Animal Fairies

Ashley the Dragon Fairy – 978-1-40830-349
Caitlin the Ice Bear Fairy – 978-1-40830-35
Erin the Firebird Fairy – 978-1-40830-351-1
Lara the Black Cat Fairy – 978-1-40830-35
Leona the Unicorn Fairy – 978-1-40830-35
Rihanna the Seahorse Fairy – 978-1-40830-
Sophia the Snow Swan Fairy – 978-140830-

The Green Fairies

Nicole the Beach Fairy – 978-1-40830-474-
Isabella the Air Fairy – 978-1-40830-475-4
Edie the Garden Fairy – 978-1-40830-476-1
Coral the Reef Fairy – 978-1-40830-477-8
Lily the Rainforest Fairy – 978-1-40830-47
Milly the River Fairy – 978-1-40830-480-8
Carrie the Snow Cap Fairy – 978-1-40830-

Holiday Specials – three stories in one!

Holly the Christmas Fairy – 978-1-84362-661-9
Summer the Holiday Fairy – 978-1-84362-960-3
Stella the Star Fairy – 978-1-84362-869-9
Kylie the Carnival Fairy – 978-1-84616-175-9
Paige the Pantomine Fairy – 978-1-84616-209-1
Flora the Fancy Dress Fairy – 978-1-84616-505-4
Chrissie the Wish Fairy – 978-1-84616-506-1
Shannon the Ocean Fairy – 978-1-40830-025-1
Gabriella the Snow Kingdom Fairy – 978-1-40830-
Mia the Bridesmaid Fairy – 978-140830-348-1
Destiny the Pop Star Fairy – 978-1-40830-473-0